Rex

REX STOUT, the creat[or] Noblesville, Indiana, in [...] of John and Lucetta To[...] Shortly after his birth the family moved to Wakarusa, Kansas. He was educated in a country school, but by the age of nine he was recognized throughout the state as a prodigy in arithmetic. Mr. Stout briefly attended the University of Kansas but left to enlist in the navy and spent the next two years as a warrant officer on board President Theodore Roosevelt's yacht. When he left the navy in 1908, Rex Stout began to write free-lance articles and worked as a sight-seeing guide and an itinerant bookkeeper. Later he devised and implemented a school banking system that was installed in four hundred cities and towns throughout the country. In 1927 Mr. Stout retired from the world of finance and, with the proceeds from his banking scheme, left for Paris to write serious fiction. He wrote three novels that received favorable reviews before turning to detective fiction. His first Nero Wolfe novel, *Fer-de-Lance*, appeared in 1934. It was followed by many others, among them *Too Many Cooks*, *The Silent Speaker*, *If Death Ever Slept*, *The Doorbell Rang*, and *Please Pass the Guilt*, which established Nero Wolfe as a leading character on a par with Erle Stanley Gardner's famous protagonist, Perry Mason. During World War II Rex Stout waged a personal campaign against nazism as chairman of the War Writers' Board, master of ceremonies of the radio program *Speaking of Liberty*, and member of several national committees. After the war he turned his attention to mobilizing public opinion against the wartime use of thermonuclear devices, was an active leader in the Authors' Guild, and resumed writing his Nero Wolfe novels. Rex Stout died in 1975 at the age of eighty-eight. A month before his death he published his seventy-second Nero Wolfe mystery, *A Family Affair*. Ten years later a seventy-third Nero Wolfe mystery was discovered and published in *Death Times Three*.

The Rex Stout Library

REX STOUT

The Mother Hunt

Introduction
by Marilyn Wallace

BANTAM BOOKS

NEW YORK • TORONTO • LONDON • SYDNEY • AUCKLAND

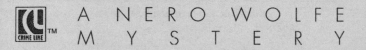

A NERO WOLFE MYSTERY

This edition contains the complete text
of the original hardcover edition.
NOT ONE WORD HAS BEEN OMITTED

THE MOTHER HUNT
A Bantam Crime Line Book / published by arrangement with
the author's estate

PUBLISHING HISTORY
Viking edition published 1963
Bantam edition / December 1981
Bantam reissue / May 1993

CRIME LINE and the portrayal of a boxed "cl" are trademarks of Bantam
Books, a division of Random House, Inc.

ISBN 0-553-24737-9

Published simultaneously in the United States and Canada

Bantam Books are published by Bantam Books, a division of Random
House, Inc. Its trademark, consisting of the words "Bantam Books" and the
portrayal of a rooster, is Registered in U.S. Patent and Trademark Office
and in other countries. Marca Registrada. Bantam Books, 1540 Broadway,
New York, New York 10036.

PRINTED IN THE UNITED STATES OF AMERICA

OPM   19   18   17   16   15   14

Introduction

I can't help it: I'm a sucker for quality and an admirer of someone who can take a set of basic materials and use simple tools to transform them into something vibrant, unique, and enduring. And that's exactly what Rex Stout has done in the Nero Wolfe series.

Even before I met him on the pages of a book fifteen years ago, I knew quite a lot about Nero Wolfe. His reputation had preceded him: he was an imposing giant of a man who holed up in a spectacular midtown Manhattan brownstone, grew orchids, was a beer aficionado . . . and he was distinctly uncomfortable in the company of women.

Despite some initial reluctance to spend a whole book's worth of time with a man who flirted with misogyny, I took the plunge. Wolfe, after all, had the good sense to live in Manhattan, and besides, you had to like a man who surrounded himself with exotic tropical plants, consumed epicurean meals, and had the chutzpah to make the universe conform to his rules. And when I met Archie Goodwin, his ebullience and his earthy, rakish charm won me over.

Hooked, I devoured as many Nero Wolfe books as I

could find in one gluttonous wintertime reading orgy. Toward the end of the tenth book I realized that, cabin fever aside, I was getting impatient. I wanted to see Wolfe shaken up a little; the man was becoming downright complacent. And in *The Mother Hunt* that's exactly what happens: Nero Wolfe not only leaves his brownstone, he actually sleeps in a strange bed in a different house. And to make matters more tenuous for the great man, he's forced into several face-to-face meetings with women.

Delicious! With these challenges to the known and predictable world, Wolfe is thrown off balance. Will he wobble into ineffectiveness? Will the resounding fall make front-page headlines in all of New York City? Devoted readers of the series grow breathless wondering about the effects of everything tossed topsy-turvy. Suspense abounds as the bodies pile up and Nero Wolfe is forced to search for a solution without the solace of his orchids and his routine, his so-very-rational thought processes in danger of being corrupted by close contact with a woman.

Wolfe, of course, declines to be undone and he triumphs. Critical to solving the case is Archie's delight in the company of women, in direct proportion to the discomfort his boss feels. From the vantage of the 1990s, Archie seems especially astute. Following a conversation with a woman, Archie observes, "Her reaction to the report had been in the groove for a woman. She had wanted to know what Carol Mardus had said, every word, and also how she had looked and how she had been dressed. There was an implication that the way she had been dressed had a definite bearing on the question, was Richard Valdon the father of the baby? but of course I let that slide. *No man with*

*any sense assumes that a woman's words mean to her
exactly what they mean to him."*

The italics are mine but the observation is pure
Archie and way ahead of its time. Not until the nineties
did gender differences in communication styles become
a hot topic. I wonder whether Rex Stout considered
himself a pioneer.

Despite Wolfe's daring foray beyond Thirty-fifth
Street, *The Mother Hunt* is really vintage Stout: lots of
grumbling and fine dining and brilliant thinking on
Wolfe's part, while Archie has a grand old time out and
about in the world. Rex Stout made the most of the
contrast between thinker and doer, achieving a delicate, ever-changing balance between the curmud-
geonly detective and his bubbly assistant. Yet just
when Wolfe seems a purely cerebral being, his physical
bulk and the very corporeal acts of eating and drinking
remind you that he is indeed a creature of the flesh.
Whenever Archie appears to be all action, chasing from
button manufacturer to baby-sitter to a beachfront rendezvous with the shapely client in the name of detec-
tion, he comes up with a brilliant ploy proving that he is
no slouch in the thinking department.

Between them, Wolfe and Archie ensure that justice
will ultimately prevail, and they do it within a classic
structure. The reader in me recognizes that the opening of *The Mother Hunt* is a staple of private-eye
fiction, the ending a fixture of the "cozy village" mystery. The book begins with a client coming to Wolfe for
help, and at once questions arise. Is she all that she
seems, or is there a womanly abundance of secrets
lurking in her past? Does she really want a solution to
the question she hired Wolfe to answer, or is she after
something else? Given Wolfe's feelings about women,

it's easy to project duplicity all over the place. And after a Wolfe-thinks–Archie-does investigation, the final scene gathers the suspects together for a drawing-room confrontation/revelation.

The writer in me admires Rex Stout's ability to shape those elements into something uniquely his.

I understood something about Rex Stout's skill as a writer when I had the personal good fortune to meet one of his daughters, Rebecca Stout Bradbury, a warm, intelligent woman with a forthright gaze and a gracious charm that immediately put me at my ease. During the morning I spent with her, we talked about her father, our own children, and the state of the American economy. And she showed me several pieces of furniture—a desk and a dresser stand out in my memory—that her father had made.

The wood was so smooth it glowed with a burnished light. Strong and true joints (no nails used here!) held together the graceful, sturdy pieces, carefully crafted and lovingly made. When I was in school, girls took home ec. while boys went to shop. Harder, more mysterious than French toast, for sure, making furniture still seems to me to be just short of magic. The rightness of each element contributes to a whole somehow greater, more pleasing in its finished state than its parts would suggest.

The same can be said of Rex Stout's mysteries, I realized on my way home that day. He chose his materials with care—characters with zest and a good share of quirky charm; a setting so palpable and familiar you can practically smell it; plots that play on readers' assumptions—and he crafted them with the same attention to detail, sure hand, and joy in the act of creation that it takes to make fine furniture.

Lingering visions of rolltop desks and dressers with hidden jewelry compartments danced in my head as I drove home. And inspiration struck as I walked in my front door and nearly tripped over one of the piles of books that seem to sprout everywhere in my house.

Aha, I thought, maybe Rex Stout would have suggested a little extracurricular woodshop: learn how to make mortise-and-tenon joints for a new set of bookcases and thicken my plot at the same time. . . .

Chapter 1

When the doorbell rang a little after eleven that Tuesday morning in early June and I went to the hall and took a look through the one-way glass panel in the front door, I saw what, or whom, I expected to see: a face a little too narrow, gray eyes a little too big, and a figure a little too thin for the best curves. I knew who it was because she had phoned Monday afternoon for an appointment, and I knew what she looked like because I had seen her a few times at theaters or restaurants.

Also I had known enough about her, part public record and part hearsay, to brief Nero Wolfe without doing any research. She was the widow of Richard Valdon, the novelist, who had died some nine months ago—drowned in somebody's swimming pool in Westchester—and since four of his books had been best sellers and one of them, *Never Dream Again*, had topped a million copies at $5.95, she should have no trouble paying a bill from a private detective if and when she got one. After reading *Never Dream Again*, five or six years ago, Wolfe had chucked it by giving it to a library, but he had thought better of a later one, *His*

Own Image, and it had a place on the shelves. Presumably that was why he took the trouble to lift his bulk from the chair when I ushered her to the office, and to stand until she was seated in the red leather chair near the end of his desk. As I went to my desk and sat I was not agog. She had said on the phone that she wanted to consult Wolfe about something very personal and confidential, but she didn't look as if she were being pinched where it hurt. It would probably be something routine like an anonymous letter or a missing relative.

Putting her bag on the stand at her elbow, she turned her head for a look around, stopped her big gray eyes at me for half a second as she turned back, and said to Wolfe, "My husband would have liked this room."

"M-m," Wolfe said. "I liked one of his books, with reservations. How old was he when he died?"

"Forty-two."

"How old are you?"

That was for my benefit. He had a triple conviction: that a) his animus toward women made it impossible for him to judge any single specimen; that b) I needed only an hour with any woman alive to tag her; and that c) he could help out by asking some blunt impertinent question, his favorite one being how old are you. It's hopeless to try to set him right.

At that, the way Lucy Valdon took it was a clue. She smiled and said, "Old enough, *plenty* old enough. I'm twenty-six. Old enough to know when I need help—and here I am. It's about—it's *extremely* confidential." She glanced at me.

Wolfe nodded. "It usually is. My ears are Mr. Goodwin's and his are mine, professionally. As for confidence, I don't suppose you have committed a major crime?"

She smiled again. It came quick and went quick, but

she meant it. "I wouldn't have the nerve. No, no crime. I want you to find somebody for me."

I thought, uh-huh, here we go. Cousin Mildred is missing and Aunt Amanda has asked her rich niece to hire a detective. But she went on; "It's a little—well, it's kind of fantastic. I have a baby, and I want to know who the mother is. As I said, this is confidential, but it's not really a secret. My maid and my cook know about it, and my lawyer, and two of my friends, but that's all, because I'm not sure I'm going to keep it—the baby."

Wolfe was frowning at her, and no wonder. "I'm not a judge of babies, madam."

"Of course not. What I want—but I must tell you. I've had it two weeks. Two weeks ago Sunday, May twentieth, the phone rang and I answered it, and a voice said there was something in my vestibule, and I went to look, and there it was on the floor, wrapped in a blanket. I took it in, and pinned to the blanket inside was a slip of paper." She got her bag from the stand and opened it, and by the time she had the paper out I was there to take it. A glance was enough to read what was on it, but instead of handing it to Wolfe across his desk I circled around to him for another look as he held it. It was a four-by-six piece of ordinary cheap paper, and the message on it, in five crooked lines, printed with one of those rubber-stamp outfits for kids, was brief and to the point:

MRS RICHARD VALDON THIS BABY IS FOR YOU
BECAUSE A BOY SHOULD LIVE IN HIS FATHERS
HOUSE

There were two pinholes near a corner. Wolfe put it on his desk, turned to her, and asked a question. "Indeed?"

"I don't know," she said. "Of course I don't. But it could be true."

"Is it likely or merely credible?"

"I guess it's likely." She closed the bag and returned it to the stand. "I mean it's likely that it could have happened." She gestured with the hand that sported a wedding ring. Her eyes came to me and back to Wolfe. "This is in confidence, you know."

"Yes."

"Well . . . since I'm telling you I want you to understand. Dick and I were married two years ago—it will be two years next month. We were in love, I still think we were, but I admit that for me there was this too, that he was a famous man, that I would be Mrs. Richard Valdon. And for him there was my—well, who I was. I was an Armstead. I didn't know how much that meant to him until after we were married, when he realized that I was sick and tired of being an Armstead."

She took a breath. "He had a sort of a Don Juan reputation before he married me, but it was probably exaggerated—those things often are. For two months we were completely . . ." She stopped and her eyes closed. In a moment they opened. "There was nothing for me but *us*, and I think for him too. I'm *sure*. After that I simply don't know, I only know it wasn't the same. During that year, the last year of his life, he may have had one woman, or two, or a dozen—I just don't know. He *could* have had, I know that. So the baby— what did I say? It's likely that it could have happened. You understand?"

Wolfe nodded. "So far. And your problem?"

"The baby, of course. I intended to have one, or two or three, I sincerely did, and Dick wanted to, but I wanted to wait. I put it off. When he died that was hard, maybe the hardest, that he had wanted me to have a baby and I had put it off. Now there is one, and I have it." She pointed at the slip of paper on Wolfe's desk. "I think what that says is right. I think a boy should live in his father's house, and certainly he should have his father's name. But the problem is, was Richard Valdon this baby's father?" She gestured. "There!"

Wolfe snorted. "Pfui. Never to be solved and you know it. Homer said it: no man can know who was his father. Shakespeare said it: it is a wise father that knows his own child. I can't help you, madam. No one can."

She smiled. "I can say 'pfui' too. Of course you can help me. I know you can't prove that Dick was the father, but you can find out who put the baby in my vestibule, and who its mother is, and then we can— Here." She got her bag and opened it. "I have figured it out." She produced another slip of paper, not the same size or kind. "The doctor said the baby was four months old, that evening, the day it came, May twentieth, so I used that date." She looked at the paper. "So it was born about January twentieth, so it was conceived about April twentieth, last year. When you know who the mother is you can find out about her and Dick, how sure it is, or anyway how likely it is, that they were together then. That won't prove this baby is his son, but it can come close—close enough. And besides, if it's just a trick, if Dick wasn't the father and couldn't have been, and you find that out, that would help me, wouldn't it? So the first thing is to find out who left it in my vestibule, and then who the mother is. Then I may want to ask her some questions myself, but I don't— Well, we'll see."

Wolfe was leaning back, scowling at her. It was beginning to look like a job he could refuse only with a phony excuse, and he hated to work, and the bank balance was fairly healthy. "You're assuming too much," he objected. "I'm not a magician, Mrs. Valdon."

"Of course not. But you're the best detective in the world, aren't you?"

"Probably not. The best detective in the world may be some rude tribesman with a limited vocabulary. You say your lawyer knows about the baby. Does he know you are consulting me?"

"Yes, but he doesn't approve. He thinks it's foolish to want to keep it. There are laws about it and he has attended to that so I can keep it temporarily, because I insisted, but he's against my trying to find the mother. But that's *my* business. His business is just the law."

Though she didn't know it, that was a hit. Wolfe couldn't have described his own attitude toward lawyers any better himself, with all his vocabulary. He let up a little on the scowl. "I doubt," he said, "if you have sufficiently considered the difficulties. The inquiry would almost certainly be prolonged, laborious, and expensive, and possibly fruitless."

"Yes. I said, I know you're not a magician."

"Can you afford it? My fees are not modest."

"I know that. I have an inheritance from my grandmother, and the income from my husband's books. I own my house." She smiled. "If you want to see a copy of my income-tax report my lawyer has it."

"Not necessary. It could take a week, a month, a year."

"All right. My lawyer says keeping the baby on a temporary basis can be extended a month at a time."

Wolfe picked up the slip of paper, glared at it, put it

down, and moved the glare to her. "You should have come to me sooner, if at all."

"I didn't decide to until yesterday, definitely."

"Possibly too late. Sixteen days have passed since Sunday, May twentieth. Was it daylight when the phone call came?"

"No, in the evening. A little after ten o'clock."

"Male voice or female?"

"I'm not sure. I think it was a man trying to sound like a woman or a woman trying to sound like a man, I don't know which."

"If you had to guess?"

She shook her head. "I can't even guess."

"What was said? Verbatim."

"I was alone in the house because the maid was out. When I answered the phone I said, 'Mrs. Valdon's residence.' The voice said, 'Is this Mrs. Valdon?' and I said yes, and the voice said, "Look in your vestibule, there's something there,' and hung up. I went down to the vestibule, and there it was. When I saw it was a live baby I took it in and called my doctor and—"

"If you please. Had you been in the house all day and evening?"

"No. I had been in the country for the weekend. I got home around eight o'clock. I hate Sunday traffic after dark."

"Where in the country?"

"Near Westport. At Julian Haft's place—he publishes my husband's books."

"Where is Westport?"

Her eyes widened a little in surprise. Mine didn't. What he doesn't know about the metropolitan area would fill an atlas. "Why, Connecticut," she said. "Fairfield County."

"What time did you leave there?"

"A little after six o'clock."

"Driving? Your own car?"

"Yes."

"With a chauffeur?"

"No. I have no chauffeur."

"Was anyone with you in the car?"

"No, I was alone." She gestured with the wedding-ring hand. "Of course you're a detective, Mr. Wolfe, I'm not, but I don't see the point of all this."

"Then you haven't used your brain." He turned. "Tell her, Archie."

He was insulting her. Not caring to bother with something so obvious, he switched it to me. I obliged. "You've probably been too busy with the baby to go into it," I told her. "Say it was me. I put the baby in the vestibule before I phoned you. I wouldn't have done that if I hadn't known you were there, that the phone would be answered. It's possible that I had hung around until I saw you come home or until I saw a light in the house, but it's even more possible that I knew you were away for the weekend and would get home by dark. I might even have known what time you left Westport. Take the last question: was anyone with you in the car? That would have been the simplest and surest way for me to know when you got home, to be with you in the car. So if you had said yes, the next question would have been, who?"

"Good heavens." She was staring at me. "Someone I know well enough to . . ." She let it hang and turned to Wolfe. "All right. Ask anything you want to."

He grunted. "Not want. Must—if I take the job. You own your house. Where is it?"

"Eleventh Street near Fifth Avenue. I inherited it.

My great-grandfather built it. When I said I was sick and tired of being an Armstead I wasn't just talking, I meant it, but I like the house, and Dick loved it."

"Do you share it? Have you any tenants?"

"No. Now I may—I don't know."

"Do the maid and the cook live there?"

"Yes."

"Any others?"

"Not living in. A woman comes five days a week to help."

"Could the maid or the cook have had a baby in January?"

She smiled. "Certainly not the cook. Nor the maid either. She has been with me nearly two years. No, she hasn't had a baby."

"Then a relative of one of them. Perhaps a sister. An ideal arrangement for an inconvenient infant nephew." Wolfe moved a hand to put it aside. "That will be routine." He tapped the slip of paper with a fingertip. "The pinholes. Was it a safety pin?"

"No, it wasn't. Just an ordinary pin."

"Indeed." His brows went up . "You said inside the blanket. Where? Near what part of the body—feet, middle, head?"

"I think the feet, but I'm not sure. I had the baby out of the blanket before I saw the paper."

Wolfe swiveled. "Archie. You like to give an opinion in terms of odds. What odds that no woman would so expose a baby to a bare pin?"

I took three seconds. "Not enough data. Exactly where was the pin? What did the baby have on? How accessible was a safety pin? Roughly, say ten to one, but that doesn't mean that one will get you ten that it was a man. I'm merely answering a question. No bet."

"I didn't invite one." He swiveled back to her. "I don't suppose it was naked in the blanket?"

"Oh no. It was dressed—too much. A sweater, a corduroy hat, corduroy overalls, a T-shirt, an undershirt, rubber pants, and diaper. Oh, and booties. It was dressed all right."

"Any safety pins?"

"Certainly, in the diaper."

"Was the diaper—uh—fresh?"

"No. It was a mess. It had probably been on for hours. I changed it before the doctor came, but I had to use a pillow case."

I cut in. "A bet, since you asked my opinion. One will get you twenty that if a woman pinned the paper to the blanket, it wasn't the one who dressed him."

No comment. He turned his head for a look at the wall clock. An hour till lunch. He took in through his nose all the air he had room for, which was plenty, let it out through his mouth, and turned to her. "It would be necessary to get more information from you, much more, and Mr. Goodwin can do that as well as I. My commitment would be to learn the identity of the mother and establish it to your satisfaction, and to demonstrate the degree of probability that your husband was the father, with no warranty of success. Is that correct?"

"Why . . . yes. If you— No, I'll just say yes."

"Very well. There's the formality of a retainer."

"Of course." She reached for her bag. "How much?"

"No matter." He pushed back his chair and rose. "A dollar, a hundred, a thousand. Mr. Goodwin will have many questions. You will excuse me."

He crossed to the door and in the hall turned left, toward the kitchen. Lunch was to be shad roe in casserole, one of the few dishes on which he and Fritz had a difference of opinion that had never been settled. They were agreed on the larding, the anchovy butter, the chervil, shallot, parsley, bay leaf, pepper, marjoram, and cream, but the argument was the onion. Fritz was for it and Wolfe dead against. There was a chance that voices would be raised, and before I got my notebook and started in on the client I went and closed the door, which was soundproofed, and on my way back to my desk she handed me a check for one thousand and 00/100 dollars.

Chapter 2

At a quarter to five that afternoon I was in conference, in the kitchen of Lucy Valdon's house on West Eleventh Street. I was standing, leaning against the refrigerator, with a glass of milk in my hand. Mrs. Vera Dowd, the cook, who evidently ate her full share of what she cooked, judging by her dimensions, was on a chair. She had supplied the milk on request. Miss Marie Foltz, the maid, in uniform, who had undoubtedly been easy to look at ten years ago and was still no eyesore, was standing across from me with her back to the sink.

"I need some help," I said and took a sip of milk.

I'm not skipping my session with the client before lunch in order to hold something back, but there's no point in reporting everything I put in my notebook. A few samples, taking her word for it:

No one hated her, or had it in for her, enough to play a dirty trick like saddling her with a loose baby—including her family. Her father and mother were in Hawaii, a stopover on an around-the-world trip; her married brother lived in Boston and her married sister in Washington. Her best friend, Lena Guthrie, one of the only three people to whom she had shown the paper that had been pinned to the blanket, the other two being the doctor and the lawyer, thought the baby looked like Dick, but she, Lucy, was reserving her opinion. She wasn't going to name the baby unless she decided to keep it. She might name it Moses because no one knew for sure who Moses' father was, but a smile went with that. And so on. Also a couple of dozen names—the names of the five other weekend guests at the Haft place in Westport on May 20, the names of four women, which I had to drag out of her, with whom Dick might possibly have played house in April 1961, and an assortment of names, mostly men, who might know more about Dick's personal diversions than his widow did. Three of those were marked as the most promising: Leo Bingham, television producer; Willis King, literary agent; and Julian Haft, publisher, the head of Parthenon Press. That's enough samples.

I was having my conference with Mrs. Dowd and Miss Foltz in the kitchen because talking comes easier to people in a room where they are used to talking. When I told them I needed some help Mrs. Dowd narrowed her eyes at me and Miss Foltz looked skeptical.

"It's about the baby," I said and took another sip of milk. "Mrs. Valdon took me upstairs for a look at it. To me it looks too fat and kind of greasy, and its nose is just a blob, but of course I'm a man."

Miss Foltz folded her arms. Mrs. Dowd said, "It's a good enough baby."

"I suppose so. Apparently whoever left it in the vestibule had the idea that Mrs. Valdon might keep it. Whether she does or not, naturally she wants to know where it came from, so she has hired a detective to find out. His name is Nero Wolfe. You may have heard of him."

"Is he on TV?" Miss Foltz inquired.

"Don't be silly," Mrs. Dowd told her. "How could he be? He's real." To me: "Certainly I've heard of him, and you too. Your picture was in the paper about a year ago. I forget your first name—no, I don't. Archie. Archie Goodwin. I should have remembered when Mrs. Valdon said Goodwin. I have a good memory for names *and* faces."

"You sure have." I sipped milk. "Here's why I need help. In a case like this, what would a detective think of first? He would think there must be some reason why the baby was left at this house instead of some other house, and what could the reason be? Well, one good reason could be that someone who lives here wants that baby to live here too. So Mr. Wolfe asked Mrs. Valdon who lives here besides her, and she said Mrs. Vera Dowd and Miss Marie Foltz, and he asked her if one of them could have had a baby about four months ago, and she said—"

They both interrupted. I raised a hand, palm out. "Now you see," I said, not raising my voice. "You see why I need help. I merely tell you a detective asked a natural and normal question, and you fly off the handle. Try being detectives yourselves once. Of course Mrs. Valdon said that neither of you could have had a baby four months ago, and the next question was, did either of you have a relative, maybe a sister, who might have had a baby she couldn't keep? That's harder to answer. I'd have to dig. I'd have to find your relatives and friends and ask a lot of questions, and that would take time and cost money, but I'd get the answer, that's sure."

"You can get the answer right now," Mrs. Dowd said.

I nodded. "I know I can, and I want it. The point is, I don't want you to hold it against Mrs. Valdon that she asked you to have a talk with me. When you hire a detective you have to let him detect. She either had to let me do this or fire Nero Wolfe. If one of you knows where the baby came from and you want it to be provided for, just say so. Mrs. Valdon may not keep it herself, but she'll see that it gets a good home, and nobody will know anything you don't want them to know. The alternative is that I'll have to start digging, seeing your relatives and friends, and finding out—"

"You don't have to see *my* relatives and friends," Mrs. Dowd said emphatically.

"Mine either," Miss Foltz declared.

I knew I didn't. Of course you can't always get a definite answer just by watching a face, but sometimes you can, and I had it. Neither of those faces had behind it the problem: to consider the offer from Mrs. Valdon, or to let me start digging. I told them so. As I finished the glass of milk I discussed faces with them, and I told them that I had assured Mrs. Valdon that a talk with them would settle it as far as they were concerned, which was a lie. You can't know what a talk is going to settle until you have had it, even when you do all the talking yourself. We parted friends, more or less.

There was an elevator, smoother and quieter than the one in Wolfe's old brownstone on West 35th Street, but it was only one flight up to where Mrs. Valdon had said she would be, and I hoofed it. It was a large room, bigger than our office and front room combined, with nothing modern in it except the carpet and a television cabinet at the far end. Everything else was probably period, but I am not up on periods. The client was on a couch, with a magazine, and nearby was a portable bar that had not been there an hour ago. She had changed again. For her appointment with Wolfe she had worn a tailored suit, tan with brown stripes; on my arrival she had had on a close-fitting gray dress that went with her eyes better than tan; now it was a lower-cut sleeveless number, light blue, apparently silk, though now you never know. She put the magazine down as I approached.

"All clear," I told her. "They're crossed off."

"You're sure?"

"Positive."

Her head was tilted back. "It didn't take you long. How did you do it?"

"Trade secret. I'm not supposed to tell a client about an operation until I have reported to Mr. Wolfe. But they took it fine. You still have a maid and a cook. If we get any ideas I may phone you in the morning."

"I'm going to have a martini. Won't you? Or what?"

Having looked at my watch as I left the kitchen, and knowing that Wolfe's afternoon session with the orchids would keep him up in the plant rooms until six o'clock, and remembering that one of my functions was to understand any woman we were dealing with, and seeing that the gin was Follansbee's, I thought I might as well be sociable. I offered to make, saying I favored five to one, and she said all right. When I had made and served and sat, on the couch beside her, and we had sampled, she said, "I want to try something. You take a sip of mine and I'll take a sip of yours. Do you mind?"

Of course I didn't, since the idea was to understand her. She held her glass for me to sip, and I held mine for her.

"Actually," I said, "this good gin is wasted on me. I just had a glass of milk."

She didn't hear me. She didn't even know I had spoken. She was looking at me but not seeing me. How was I to understand that? Not wanting to sit and stare at her, I moved my eyes to her shoulder and arm, which weren't really skinny.

"I don't know why I suddenly wanted to do that," she said. "I haven't done it since Dick died. I've never done it with anybody but him. All of a sudden I knew I had to try it, I don't know why."

It seemed advisable to keep it professional, and the simplest way was to bring Wolfe in. "Mr. Wolfe says," I told her, "that nobody ever gets to the real why of anything."

She smiled. "And upstairs, when you were looking at the baby, I nearly called you Archie. I'm not trying to flirt with you. I don't know how to flirt. I don't suppose— You're not a hypnotist, are you?"

I sipped the martini. "What the hell," I said. "Relax. Exchanging sips is an old Persian custom. As for calling me Archie, that's my name. Don't call me Svengali. As for flirting, let's discuss it. Men and women flirt. Horses flirt. Parakeets flirt. Undoubtedly oysters flirt, but they must have some special—"

I stopped because she was moving. She left the couch, went and put the glass, still half full, on the bar, turned, and said, "Don't forget the suitcase when you go," and walked out.

That took some fancy understanding. I sat and worked on it while I finished the martini, four or five minutes, got up and put my glass on the bar, touching hers to show I understood, which I didn't, and departed. In the lower hall, on my way out, I picked up the small suitcase which she had helped me pack.

At that time of day getting a taxi in that part of town is like expecting to draw a ten to an eight, nine, jack, and queen, and it was only twenty-four short blocks and four long ones, and the suitcase was light. Anyway I'm a walker. I wanted to make it before Wolfe got down to the office, and did; it was 5:54 when I mounted the stoop of the old brownstone, used my key, entered, went to the office, put the suitcase on my chair, and unpacked. By the time the sound of the elevator came, all the items were spread out on Wolfe's desk, just about covering it, and when he walked in I was at my desk, busy with papers. When he stopped and let out a growl I swiveled.

"What the devil is this?" he demanded.

I arose and pointed. "Sweater. Hat. Overalls. T-shirt. Undershirt. Blanket. Booties. Rubber pants. Diaper. You have to hand it to her for keeping the diaper. The maid wasn't there and she didn't get a nurse until the next day. She must have washed it herself. There are no laundry marks or store labels. The sweater, hat, overalls, and booties have brand labels, but I doubt if they will help. There's something about one item that might possibly help. If you don't spot it yourself it may not be worth mentioning."

He went to his made-to-order chair and sat. "The maid and the cook?"

"We had a conference. They're out. Do you want it verbatim?"

"Not if you're satisfied."

"I am. Of course if we draw nothing but blanks we can check on them."

"What else?"

"First, there is a live baby. I saw it. She didn't just dream it. There's nothing unusual about the vestibule; the door has no lock and it's only four steps up, anyone could pop in and out; trying to find someone who saw somebody doing so seventeen days ago after dark would be a waste of my time and the client's money. I didn't include the cleaning woman in the conference because if the baby was hers it would be a different color, and I didn't include the nurse because she was hired through an agency the next day. There's a fine Tekke rug in the nursery, which was a spare bedroom. You are aware that I know about rugs from you, and about pictures from Miss Rowan. There's a Renoir in the living room, and I think a Cézanne. The client uses Follansbee gin. I am in bad with her because I forgot she's an Armstead and used a little profanity. She'll sleep it off."

"Why the profanity?"

"She jiggled my arm and I spilled gin on my pants."

He eyed me. "You had better report verbatim."

"Not necessary. I'm satisfied."

"No doubt. Have you any suggestions?"

"Yes, sir. It looks pretty hopeless. If we get nowhere in a couple of weeks you can tell her you have discovered that it's my baby, I put it in the vestibule, and if she'll marry me she can keep it. As for the mother, I can simply—"

"Shut up."

I hadn't decided how to handle the mother question anyway. He picked up the sweater and inspected it. I sat, leaned back, crossed my legs, and looked on. He didn't turn the sweater inside out, so this was just a once-over and he would go back to it. He put it down and picked up the hat. When he got to the overalls I watched his face but saw no sign that he had noticed anything, and I swiveled and reached to the rack of phone books for the Manhattan Yellow Pages, formerly the Red Book. I found what I was after, under Children's & Infants' Wear—Whol. & Mfrs., which filled four and a half pages. I started a hand for the phone, but drew it back. He might spot it the second time around and should have the chance without a tip from me. I got up and went to the hall and up two flights to my room, and at the phone on my bedstand I dialed the number, but got what was to be expected at that time of day, no answer. I tried another number, a woman I knew who was the mother of three young ones, and got her, but she was no help; she said she would have to see the overalls. So it would have to wait until morning. I went back down to the office.

Wolfe had turned his chair and was holding the overalls up to get the full light, and in his other hand was his biggest magnifying glass. He was examining a button. As I crossed to him I asked, "Find something?"

He swiveled and put the glass down. "Possibly. The buttons on this garment. Four of them."

"What about them?"

"They seem inappropriate. Such garments must be made by the million, including the buttons. But these buttons were surely not mass-produced. The material looks like horsehair, white horsehair, though I presume it could be one of the synthetic fibers. But there is considerable variation in size and shape. They couldn't possibly have been made in large quantities by a machine."

I sat. "That's very interesting. Congratulations."

"I suggest you examine them."

"I already have, not with a glass. Of course you saw

that the brand label of the overalls is Cherub. That brand is made by Resnick and Spiro, Three-forty West Thirty-seventh Street. I just dialed their number but got no answer, since it's after six. A five-minute walk from here in the morning, unless you want me to find Mr. Resnick or Mr. Spiro now."

"The morning will do. Should I apologize for pulling a feather from your cap?"

"We'll split it," I said and rose to get the overalls and the glass.

Chapter 3

The Manhattan garment district has got everything from thirty-story marble palaces to holes
in the wall. It is no place to go for a stroll, because
you are off the sidewalk most of the time, detouring
around trucks that are backed in or headed in, but it's
fine as a training ground for jumping and dodging, and
as a refresher for reflexes. If you can come out whole
from an hour in those cross streets in the Thirties you'll
be safe anywhere in the world. So I felt I had accomplished something when I walked into the entrance of
340 West 37th Street at ten o'clock Wednesday morning.

But then it got complicated. I tried my best to explain, first to a young woman at a window on the first
floor and then to a man in an anteroom on the fourth
floor, but they simply couldn't understand, if I didn't
want to sell something or buy something, and wasn't
looking for a job, why I was in the building. I finally
made it in to a man at a desk who had a broader outlook.
Naturally he couldn't see why the question, had those
buttons been put on those overalls by Resnick & Spiro?
was important enough for me to fight my way through

37th Street to get it answered, but he was too busy to go into that. It was merely that he realized that a man who had gone to so much trouble to ask him a question deserved an answer. After one quick look he said that Resnick & Spiro had never used such a button and never would. They used plastic almost exclusively. He handed me the overalls.

"Many thanks," I said. "Why I'm bothering about this wouldn't interest you, but it's not just curiosity. Do you know of any firm that makes buttons like these?"

He shook his head. "No idea."

"Have you ever seen any buttons like them?"

"Never."

"Could you tell me what they're made of?"

He leaned over for another look. "My guess would be some synthetic, but God only knows." Suddenly he smiled, wide, human, and humorous. "Or maybe the Emperor of Japan does. Try him. Pretty soon everything will come from there."

I thanked him, stuffed the overalls back in the paper bag, and departed. Having suspected that that would be all I would get from Resnick & Spiro, I had spent an hour Tuesday evening with the Yellow Pages, the four and a half pages of listings under Buttons, and in my pocket notebook were the names of fifteen firms within five blocks of where I was. One was only fifty paces down the street, and I headed for it.

Ninety minutes later, after calling on four different firms, I knew a little more about buttons in general, but still nothing specific about the ones on the overalls. One of the firms made covered buttons, another polyester and acrylic, another freshwater and ocean pearl, another gold and silver plated. Nobody had any notion who had made mine or what they were made of, and nobody cared. It was looking as if all I would get was a collection of negatives, which was all right in a way, as I walked down the hall on the sixth floor of a building on 39th Street to a door that was lettered: EXCLUSIVE NOVELTY BUTTON CO.

That was where I would have gone first if I had known. A woman who knew exactly what I was after before I said ten words took me to an inner room which had no racks on the walls, not a button in sight. A little old geezer with big ears and a mop of white hair, sitting at a table looking at a portfolio, didn't look up until I was beside him and had the overalls out of the bag, and when his eyes moved they lit on one of the buttons. He jerked the overalls out of my hands, squinted at each of the buttons in turn, the two on the bib and the two at the sides, raised his eyes to me, and demanded, "Where did these buttons come from?"

I laughed. It may not strike you as funny, but that was the question I had been working on for nearly two hours. There was a chair there and I took it. "I'm laughing at me, not you," I told him. "A definite answer to that question is worth a hundred dollars, cash, to anyone who has it. I won't explain why, it's too complicated. Can you answer it?"

"Are you a button man?"

"No."

"Who are you?"

I got my case from my pocket and produced a card. He took it and squinted at it. "You're a private detective?"

"Right."

"Where did you get these buttons?"

"Listen," I said, "I only want to—"

"*You* listen, young man. I know more about buttons

than any man in the world. I get them from everywhere. I have the finest and most comprehensive collection in existence. Also I sell them. I have sold a thousand dozen buttons in one lot for forty cents a dozen, and I have sold four buttons for six thousand dollars. I have sold buttons to the Duchess of Windsor, to Queen Elizabeth, and to Miss Bette Davis. I have given buttons to nine different museums in five countries. I know absolutely that no man could show me a button that I couldn't place, but you have done so. Where did you get them?"

"All right," I said, "I listened, now it's your turn. I know less about buttons than any man in the world. In connection with a case I'm working on I need to know where those overalls came from. Since they're a standard product, sold everywhere, they can't be traced, but it seemed to me that the buttons are not standard and *might* be traced. That's what I'm trying to find out, where they came from. Apparently you can't tell me."

"I admit I can't!"

"Okay. Obviously you know about unusual buttons, rare buttons. Do you also know about ordinary commercial buttons?"

"I know about all buttons!"

"And you have never seen buttons like these or heard of any?"

"No! I admit it!"

"Fine." I reached to a pocket for my wallet, extracted five twenties, and put them on the table. "You haven't answered my question, but you've been a big help. Is there any chance that those buttons were made by a machine?"

"No. Impossible. Someone spent hours on each one. It's a technique I have never seen."

"What are they made of? What material?"

"That may be difficult. It may take some time. I may be able to tell you by tomorrow afternoon."

"I can't wait that long." I reached for the overalls, but he didn't turn loose.

"I'd rather have the buttons than the money," he said. "Or just one of them. You don't need all four."

I had to yank to get the overalls. With them back in the bag, I stood. "You've saved me a lot of time and trouble," I told him, "and I'd like to show my appreciation. If and when I'm through with the buttons I'll donate one or more of them to your collection, and I'll tell you where they came from. I hope."

It took me five minutes to get away and out. I didn't want to be rude. He was probably the only button fiend in America, and I had been lucky enough to hit him before lunch.

A question about lunch was in my mind as I left the building. It was ten minutes past noon. Did Nathan Hirsh lunch early or late? Since I could walk it in twelve minutes I decided not to take time to phone, and again I was lucky. As I entered the anteroom of the Hirsh Laboratories on the tenth floor of a building on 43rd Street, Hirsh himself entered from within, on his way out, and when I told him I had something from Nero Wolfe that shouldn't wait he took me in and down the hall to his room. A few years back, the publicity from his testimony in court on one of Wolfe's cases hadn't hurt his business a bit.

I produced the overalls and said, "One simple little question. What are the buttons made of?"

He went to his desk for a glass and inspected one of them. "Not so simple," he said, "with all the stuff there is around. It looks like horsehair, but to be sure we'd have to rip into one of them."

"How long will it take?"

"Anywhere from twenty minutes to five hours."

I told him the sooner the better and he knew the phone number.

I got to 35th Street and into the house just as Wolfe was crossing the hall to the dining room. Since mention of business is not permitted at table, he stopped at the sill and asked, "Well?"

"Well so far," I told him. "In fact perfect. A man who knows as much about buttons as you do about food has never seen anything like them. Someone spent hours on each one of them. The material had him stumped, so I took them to Hirsh. He'll report this afternoon."

He said satisfactory and proceeded to the table, and I went to wash my hands before joining him.

With all the trick gadgets they had hatched, there may be one you could attach to Wolfe and me and find out if he riles me more than I do him or vice versa, but we haven't got one, so I don't know. I admit that there are times when there is nothing to do but wait, but the point is how you wait. In the office that day after lunch I riled Wolfe by glancing at my watch every few minutes while he was dictating a long letter to an orchid-hunter in Honduras, and then he riled me by settling back, completely at ease, with *Travels with Charley* by John Steinbeck. Damn it, he had a job. If he had to read a book, why not get *His Own Image* by Richard Valdon from the shelf? There might be some kind of a hint in it somewhere.

It was 3:43 when the phone call came from Hirsh. I had my notebook ready in case it was complicated with long scientific words, but it took only common ones and not many of them. I hung up and swiveled, and Wolfe actually moved his eyes from the book.

"Horsehair," I said. "No dye or lacquer or anything, just plain unadulterated white horsehair."

He grunted. "Is there time for an advertisement in tomorrow's papers? *Times* and *News* and *Gazette*."

"*Times* and *News*, maybe. *Gazette*, yes."

"Your notebook. Two columns wide, four inches or so. At the top, one hundred dollars, in figures, thirty-point or larger, boldface. Below in fourteen-point, also boldface: will be paid in cash for information regarding the maker, comma, or if not the maker the source, comma, of buttons made by hand of white horsehair. Period. Buttons of any size or shape suitable for use on clothing. Period. I want to know, comma, not who might make such buttons, comma, but who has actually done so. Period. The hundred dollars will be paid only to the person who first supplies the information. At the bottom, my name, address, and telephone number."

"Boldface?"

"No. Standard weight, condensed."

As I turned and reached for the typewriter I would have given a dozen polyester buttons to know whether he had planned it while he was dictating letters or while he was reading *Travels with Charley*.

Chapter 4

The house rules in the old brownstone on West 35th Street are of course set by Wolfe, since he owns the house, but any variation in the morning routine usually comes from me. Wolfe sticks to his personal schedule: at 8:15 breakfast in his room on the second floor, on a tray taken up by Fritz, at nine o'clock to the elevator and up to the plant rooms, and down to the office at eleven. My schedule depends on what is stirring and on what time I turned in. I need to be flat a full eight hours, and at night I adjust the clock on my bedstand accordingly; and since I spent that Wednesday evening at a theater, and then at the Flamingo, with a friend, and it was after one when I got home, I set the pointer at 9:30.

But it wasn't the radio, nudged by the clock, that roused me Thursday morning. When it happened I squeezed my eyes tighter shut to try to figure out what the hell it was. It wasn't the phone, because I had switched my extension off, and anyway it wasn't loud enough. It was a bumblebee, and why the hell was a bumblebee buzzing around 35th Street in the middle of the night? Or maybe the sun was up. I forced my eyes open and focused on the clock. Six minutes to nine. And it was the house phone, of course, I should have known. I rolled over and reached for it.

"Archie Goodwin's room, Mr. Goodwin speaking."

"I'm sorry, Archie." Fritz. "But she insists—"

"Who?"

"A woman on the phone. Something about buttons. She says—"

"Okay, I'll take it." I flipped the switch of the extension and got the receiver. "Yes? Archie Goodwin speak—"

"I want Nero Wolfe and I'm in a hurry!"

"He's not available. If it's about the ad—"

"It is. I saw it in the *News*. I know about some buttons like that and I want to be first—"

"You are. Your name, please?"

"Beatrice Epps. E-P-P-S. Am I first?"

"You are if it fits. Mrs. Epps, or Miss?"

"Miss Beatrice Epps. I can't tell you now—"

"Where are you, Miss Epps?"

"I'm in a phone booth at Grand Central. I'm on my way to work and I have to be there at nine o'clock, so I can't tell you now, but I wanted to be first."

"Sure. Very sensible. Where do you work?"

"At Quinn and Collins in the Chanin Building. Real estate. But don't come there, they wouldn't like it. I'll phone again on my lunch hour."

"What time?"

"Half past twelve."

"Okay, I'll be at the newsstand in the Chanin Building at twelve-thirty and I'll buy you a lunch. I'll have an orchid in my buttonhole, a small one, white and green, and I'll have a hundred—"

"I'm late, I have to go. I'll be there." The connection

went. I flopped back onto the pillow, found that I was too near awake for another half-hour to be any good, swung around, and got my feet on the floor.

At ten o'clock I was in the kitchen at my breakfast table, sprinkling brown sugar on a buttered sour-milk griddle cake, with the *Times* before me on the rack. Fritz, standing by, asked, "No cinnamon?"

"No," I said firmly. "I've decided it's an aphrodisiac."

"Then for you it would be—how is it? Taking coal somewhere."

"Coals to Newcastle. That's not the point, but you mean well and I thank you."

"I always mean well." Seeing that I had taken the second bite, he stepped to the range to start the next cake. "I saw the advertisement. Also I saw the things on your desk that you brought in the suitcase. I have heard that the most dangerous kind of case for a detective is a kidnaping case."

"Maybe and maybe not. It depends."

"And in all the years I have been with him this is the first kidnaping case he has ever had."

I sipped coffee. "There you go again, Fritz, circling around. You could just ask, is it a kidnaping case? and I would say no. Because it isn't. Of course the baby clothes gave you the idea. Just between you and me, in strict confidence, the baby clothes belong to him. It isn't decided yet when the baby will move in here, and I doubt if the mother ever will, but I understand she's a good cook, and if you happen to take a long vacation . . ."

He was there with the cake and I reached for the tomato and lime marmalade. With it no butter. "You are a true friend, Archie," he said.

"They don't come any truer."

"*Vraiment.* I'm glad you told me so I can get things in. Is it a boy?"

"Yes. It looks like him."

"Good. Do you know what I will do?" He returned to the range and gestured with the cake turner. "I will put cinnamon in everything!"

I disapproved and we debated it.

Instead of waiting until Wolfe came down, to report the development, after I had done the morning chores in the office—opening the mail, dusting, emptying the wastebaskets, removing sheets from the desk calendars, putting fresh water in the vase on Wolfe's desk—I mounted the three flights to the plant rooms. June is not the best show-off month for a collection of orchids, especially not for one like Wolfe's, with more than two hundred varieties. The first room, the tropical, had only a few splotches of color; the next one, the intermediate, was more flashy but nothing like March; the third one, the cool, had more flowers but they're not so gaudy. In the last one, the potting room, Wolfe was at the bench with Theodore Horstmann, inspecting the nodes on a pseudo-bulb. As I approached he turned his head and growled, "Well?" He is supposed to be interrupted up there only in an emergency.

"Nothing urgent," I said. "Just to tell you that I'm taking a Cypripedium lawrenceanum hyeanum—one flower. To wear. A woman phoned about buttons, and when I meet her at twelve-thirty it will mark me."

"When will you leave?"

"A little before noon. I'll stop at the bank on the way to deposit a check."

"Very well." He resumed the inspection. Too busy for questions. I went and got the posy and on down. When he came down at eleven he asked for a verbatim

report and got it, and had one question: "What about
her?" I told him his guess was as good as mine, say one
chance in ten that she really had it, and when I said I
might as well leave sooner and get the overalls from
Hirsh and have them with me, he approved.

So when I took post near the newsstand in the lobby
of the Chanin Building, a little ahead of time, having
learned from the directory that Quinn and Collins was
on the ninth floor, I had the paper bag. That kind of
waiting is different, with faces to watch coming and
going, male and female, old and young, sure and saggy.
About half of them looked as if they needed either a
doctor or a lawyer or a detective, including the one who
stopped in front of me with her head tilted back. When
I said, "Miss Epps?" she nodded.

"I'm Archie Goodwin. Shall we go downstairs? I have
reserved a table."

She shook her head. "I always eat lunch alone."

I want to be fair, but it's fair to say that she had
probably had very few invitations to lunch, if any. Her
nose was flat and she had twice as much chin as she
needed. Her age was somewhere between thirty and
fifty. "We can talk here," she said.

"At least we can start here," I conceded. "What do
you know about white horsehair buttons?"

"I know I've seen some. But before I tell you—how
do I know you'll pay me?"

"You don't." I touched her elbow and we moved
aside, away from the traffic. "But I do." I got a card
from my case and handed it to her. "Naturally I'll have
to check what you tell me, and it will have to be practi-
cal. You could tell me you knew a man in Singapore who
made white horsehair buttons but he's dead."

"I've never been in Singapore. It's nothing like that."

"Good. What is it like?"

"I saw them right here. In this building."

"When?"

"Last summer." She hesitated and then went on. "There was a girl in the office for a month, vacation time, filling in, and one day I noticed the buttons on her blouse. I said I had never seen any buttons like them, and she said very few people had. I asked her where I could get some, and she said nowhere. She said her aunt made them out of horsehair, and it took her a day to make one button, so she didn't make them to sell, just as a hobby."

"Were the buttons white?"

"Yes."

"How many were on her blouse?"

"I don't remember. I think five."

At the Hirsh Laboratories, deciding it would be better not to display the overalls, I had cut off one of the buttons, one of the three still intact. I took it from a pocket and offered it. "Anything like that?"

She gave it a good look. "Exactly like that, as I remember, but of course it was nearly a year ago. That size too."

I retrieved the button. "This sounds as if it may help, Miss Epps. What's the girl's name?"

She hesitated. "I suppose I have to tell you."

"You certainly do."

"I don't want to get her into any trouble. Nero Wolfe is a detective and so are you."

"I don't want to get anybody into trouble unless they have asked for it. Anyway, from what you've already told me it would be a cinch to find her. What's her name?"

"Tenzer. Anne Tenzer."

"What's her aunt's name?"

"I don't know. She didn't tell me and I didn't ask."

"Have you seen her since last summer?"

"No."

"Do you know if Quinn and Collins got her through an agency?"

"Yes, they did. The Stopgap Employment Service."

"How old is she?"

"Oh—she's under thirty."

"Is she married?"

"No. As far as I know."

"What does she look like?"

"She's about my size. She's a blonde—or she was last summer. She thinks she's very attractive, and I guess she is. I guess you would think so."

"I'll see when I see her. Of course I won't mention you." I got my wallet out. "My instructions from Mr. Wolfe were not to pay you until I have checked your information, but he hadn't met you and heard you, and I have." I produced two twenties and a ten. "Here's half of it, with the understanding that you will say nothing about this to anyone. You impress me as a woman who can watch her tongue."

"I can."

"Say *nothing* to *anyone*. Right?"

"I won't." She put the bills in her bag. "When will I get the rest?"

"Soon. I may see you again, but if that isn't necessary I'll mail it. If you'll give me your home address and phone number?"

She did so, West 169th Street, was going to add something, decided not to, and turned to go. I watched her to the entrance. There was no spring to her legs.

The relation between a woman's face and the way she walks would take a chapter in a book I'll never write.

Since I had a table reserved in the restaurant downstairs, I went down and took it and ordered a bowl of clam chowder, which Fritz never makes, and which was all I wanted after my late breakfast. Having stopped on the way to consult the phone book, I knew the address of the Stopgap Employment Service—493 Lexington Avenue. But the approach had to be considered because (1) agencies are cagey about the addresses of their personnel, and (2) if Anne Tenzer was the mother of the baby she would have to be handled with care. I preferred not to phone Wolfe. The understanding was that when I was out on an errand I would use intelligence guided by experience (as he put it), meaning my intelligence, not his.

The result was that shortly after two o'clock I was seated in the anteroom of the Exclusive Novelty Button Co., waiting for a phone call, or rather, hoping for one. I had made a deal with Mr. Nicholas Losseff, the button fiend, as he had sat at his desk eating salami, black bread, cheese, and pickles. What he got was the button I had removed from the overalls and a firm promise to tell him the source when circumstances permitted. What I got was permission to make a phone call and wait there to get one back, no matter how long it took, and use his office for an interview if I needed to. The phone call had been to the Stopgap Employment Service. Since I had known beforehand that I might have a lot of time to kill, I had stopped on the way to buy four magazines and two paperbacks, one of the latter being *His Own Image* by Richard Valdon.

I never got to *His Own Image*, but the magazines got a big play, and I was halfway through the other paperback, a collection of pieces about the Civil War, when the phone call came at a quarter past five. The woman at the desk, who had known what I wanted Wednesday before I told her, vacated her chair for me, but I went and took it on my side, standing.

"Goodwin speaking."

"This is Anne Tenzer. I got a message to call the Exclusive Novelty Button Company and ask for Mr. Goodwin."

"Right. I'm Goodwin." Her voice had plenty of feminine in it, so I put plenty of masculine in mine. "I would like very much to see you, to get some information if possible. I think you may know something about a certain kind of button."

"Me? I don't know anything about buttons."

"I thought you might, about this particular button. It's made by hand of white horsehair."

"Oh." A pause. "Why, how on earth—do you mean you've got one?"

"Yes. May I ask, where are you?"

"I'm in a phone booth at Madison Avenue and Forty-ninth Street."

From her voice, I assumed that my voice was doing all right. "Then I can't expect you to come here to my office, Thirty-ninth Street and crosstown. How about the Churchill lobby? You're near there. I can make it in twenty minutes. We can have a drink and discuss buttons."

"You mean *you* can discuss buttons."

"Okay. I'm pretty good at it. Do you know the Blue Alcove at the Churchill?"

"Yes."

"I'll be there in twenty minutes, with no hat, a paper

bag in my hand, and a white and green orchid in my lapel."

"Not an *orchid*. Men don't wear orchids."

"I do, and I'm a man. Do you mind?"

"I won't know till I see you."

"That's the spirit. All right, I'm off."

Chapter 5

At a wall table in the Admiralty Bar at the Churchill there isn't much light, but there had been in the lobby. Beatrice Epps had been correct when she said Anne Tenzer was about her size, but the resemblance stopped there. It was quite conceivable that Miss Tenzer had aroused in some man, possibly Richard Valdon, the kind of reaction that is an important factor in the propagation of the species; in fact, in more men than one. She was still a blonde, but she wasn't playing it up; she didn't have to. She sipped a Bloody Mary as if she could take it or leave it.

The button question had been disposed of in ten minutes. I had explained that the Exclusive Novelty Button Co. specialized in rare and unusual buttons, and that someone in one of the places she had worked had told me that she had noticed the buttons on her blouse, had asked her about them, and had been told that they had been made by hand of white horsehair. She said that was right, her aunt had made them for years as a hobby and had given her six of them as a birthday present. She still had them, five of them still on the blouse and the other one put away somewhere. She didn't remind me that I had told her on the phone that I had one. I asked if she thought her aunt had a supply of them that she might be willing to sell, and she said she didn't know but she didn't think she could have very many, because it took a whole day to make one. I asked if she would mind if I went to see her aunt to find out, and she said of course not and gave me the name and address: Miss Ellen Tenzer, Rural Route 2, Mahopac, New York. Also she gave me the phone number.

Having learned where to find the aunt, the source of the buttons, I decided to try a risky short cut with the niece. Of course it was dangerous, but it might simplify matters a lot. I smiled at her, a good masculine smile, and said, "I've held out on you a little, Miss Tenzer. I have not only heard about the buttons, I have seen some of them, and I have them with me." I put the paper bag on the table and slipped out the overalls. "There were four, but I took two off to inspect them. See?"

Her reaction settled it. It didn't prove that she had never had a baby, or that she had had no hand in dumping one in Lucy Valdon's vestibule, but it did prove that even if she had done the dumping herself, she hadn't known that the baby was wearing blue corduroy overalls with white horsehair buttons, which seemed very unlikely.

She took the overalls, looked at the buttons, and handed them back. "They're Aunt Ellen's, all right," she said. "Or a darned good imitation. Don't tell me someone told you I was wearing *that* some place where I worked. It wouldn't fit."

"Obviously," I agreed. "I showed them to you because you're being very obliging and I thought they might amuse you. I'll tell you where I got them if you're curious."

She shook her head. "Don't bother. That's one of my many shortcomings, I'm never curious about things that don't matter. I mean matter to me. Maybe you're not either. Maybe you're only curious about buttons. Haven't we had enough about buttons?"

"Plenty." I returned the overalls to the bag. "I'm like you, curious only about things that matter to me. Right now I'm curious about you. What kind of office work do you do?"

"Oh, I'm very special. Secretarial, highest type. When a private secretary gets married or goes on vacation or gets fired by her boss's wife, and there's no one else around that will do, that's for me. Have you a secretary?"

"Certainly. She's eighty years old, never takes a vacation, and refuses all offers of marriage, and I have no wife to fire her. Have you got a husband?"

"No. I had one for a year and that was too long. I didn't look before I leaped, and I'll never leap again."

"Maybe you're in a rut, secretarying for important men in offices. Maybe you ought to vary it a little, scientists or college presidents or authors. It might be interesting to work for a famous author. Have you ever thought of trying it?"

"No, I haven't. I suppose they have secretaries."

"Sure they have."

"Do you know any?"

"I know a man who wrote a book about buttons, but he's not very famous. Shall we have a refill?"

She was willing. I wasn't, but didn't say so. Expecting nothing more from her at present, I wanted to shake a leg, but she might be useful somehow in the future, and anyway I had given her the impression that she was making an impression, so I couldn't suddenly remember that I was late for an appointment. Another anyway, if one is needed: she was easy to look at and listen to, and if your intelligence is to be guided by experience you have to have experience. There were indications that an invitation to dine might be accepted, but that would have meant the whole evening and would have cost Lucy Valdon at least twenty bucks.

I got home a little after seven and, entering the office, found that I owed Wolfe an apology. He was reading *His Own Image*. He finished a paragraph and, since it was close to dinnertime, inserted his bookmark and put the book down. He never dog-ears a book that gets a place on the shelves. Many a time I have seen him use the bookmark part way and then begin dog-earing.

His look asked the question and I answered it. He wants a verbatim report only when nothing less will do, so I merely gave him the facts, of course including Anne Tenzer's reaction to the overalls. When I finished he said, "Satisfactory." Then he decided that was an understatement and added, "Very satisfactory."

"Yes, sir," I agreed. "I could use a raise."

"No doubt. Of course you have considered the possibility that she had seen the advertisement, knew you were shamming, and was gulling you."

I nodded. "Any odds you want she hadn't seen the ad. She did no fishing, and she isn't dumb."

"Where's Mahopac?"

"Sixty miles north. Putnam County. I can grab a bite in the kitchen and be there by nine o'clock."

"No. The morning will do. You're impetuous." He looked at the wall clock. Fritz would come any minute to announce dinner. "Can you get Saul now?"

"Why?" I demanded. "I didn't say I would quit if I didn't get a raise. I merely said I could use one."

He grunted. "And I said no doubt. You will go to Mahopac in the morning. Meanwhile Saul will learn what Miss Tenzer, the niece, was doing in January. Could she have given birth to that baby? You think not, but it's just as well to make sure, and Saul can do it without—" He turned his head. Fritz was in the doorway.

Since Saul has been mentioned I might as well introduce him. Of the three free-lance ops we call on when we need help, Saul Panzer is the pick. If you included everybody in the metropolitan area, he would still be the pick, which is why, though his price is ten dollars an hour, he is offered five times as many jobs as he takes. If and when you need a detective and only the second best will do, get him if you can. For the best, Nero Wolfe, it's more like ten dollars a minute.

So Friday morning, a fine bright morning, worth noticing even for early June, as I rolled along the Sawmill River Parkway in the Heron sedan, which belongs to Wolfe but is used by me, I had no worries behind me, since it was Saul who was checking on Anne Tenzer. If necessary he could find out where and when she ate lunch on January 17, whether anybody remembered or not, without getting anybody curious or stirring up any dust. That may sound far-fetched, and it is, but he is unquestionably a seventh son or something.

It was 10:35 when I turned the Heron in to a filling station on the edge of Mahopac, stopped, got out, walked over to a guy who was cleaning a customer's windshield, and asked if he knew where Miss Ellen Tenzer lived. He said he didn't but the boss might, and I went inside and found the boss, who was about half the age of his hired help. He knew exactly where Ellen Tenzer lived and told me how to get there. From his tone and manner it was obvious that there was practically nothing he didn't know, and he could probably have answered questions about her, but I didn't ask any. It's a good habit to limit your questions to what you really need.

Another chapter of the book I'll never write would be on how to give directions to places. Turning right at the church was fine, but in about a mile there was a fork he hadn't mentioned. I stopped the car, fished for a quarter, looked at it, saw tails, and went left. That way you're not responsible for a bum guess. The coin was right, for in another mile I came to the bridge he *had* mentioned, and a little farther on the dead end, where I turned right. Pretty soon the blacktop stopped and I was on gravel, curving and sloping up with woods on both sides, and in half a mile there was her mailbox on the left. I turned in, to a narrow driveway with ruts, took it easy not to bump trees, and was at the source of the white horsehair buttons. When I got out I left the paper bag with the overalls in the glove compartment. I might want them and I might not.

I glanced around. Woods on all sides. For my taste, too many trees and too close to the house. The clearing was only sixty paces long and forty wide, and the graveled turnaround was barely big enough. The overhead door of a one-car garage was open and the car was there, a Rambler sedan. The garage was connected to the house, one story, the boarding of which ran up and down instead of horizontal and had grooves, and was painted white. The paint was as good as new, and everything was clean and neat, including the flower beds. I headed for the door, and it opened before I reached it.

A disadvantage of not wearing a hat is that you can't take it off when you meet a nice little middle-aged lady, or perhaps nearer old than middle-aged, with gray hair bunched in a neat topknot and gray eyes clear and alive. When I said, "Miss Ellen Tenzer?" she nodded and said, "That's my name."

"Mine's Goodwin. I suppose I should have phoned, but I was glad to have an excuse to drive to the country on such a fine day. I'm in the button business, and I understand you are too in a way—well, not the *business*. I'm interested in the horsehair buttons you make. May I come in?"

"Why are you interested in them?"

That struck me as slightly off key. It would have been more natural for her to say How do you know I make horsehair buttons? or Who told you I make horsehair buttons?

"Well," I said, "I suppose you would like me better if I pretended it's art for art's sake, but as I said, I'm in the button business, and I specialize in buttons that are different. I thought you might be willing to let me have some. I would pay a good price, cash."

Her eyes went to the Heron and back to me. "I only have a few. Only seventeen."

Still no curiosity about where I had heard of them. Maybe, like her niece, she was curious only about things that mattered to her. "That would do for a start," I said. "Would it be imposing on you to ask for a drink of water?"

"Why—no." She moved, and with the doorway free I entered, and as she crossed to another door at the left I advanced and used my eyes. I have good eyes, plenty good enough to recognize from six yards away an object I had seen before—or rather, one just like it. It was on a table between two windows at the opposite wall, and it changed the program completely as far as Ellen Tenzer was concerned. It had been quite possible, even probable, that the buttons on the overalls were some she had given to somebody, maybe years ago, but not now. Perhaps still possible, but just barely.

Not wanting her to know I had spotted it, I headed for the door she had left by and went through to the kitchen. At the sink with the faucet running, she filled a glass and offered it, and I took it and drank. "Good water," I said. "A deep well?"

She didn't answer. Probably she hadn't heard my question, since she had one of her own on her mind. She asked it: "How did you find out I make buttons?"

Worded wrong and too late. If she had asked it sooner, and if I hadn't seen the object on the table, I would have had to answer it as I had intended. I emptied the glass and put it down and said, "Thank you very much. Wonderful water. How I found out is kind of complicated, and it doesn't matter, does it? May I see some of them?"

"I told you, I only have seventeen."

"I know, but if you don't mind . . ."

"What did you say your name is?"

"Goodwin. Archie Goodwin."

"All right, you've had your drink of water, now you can go."

"But Miss Tenzer, I've driven sixty miles just to—"

"I don't care if you've driven six hundred miles. I'm not going to show you any buttons and I'm not going to talk about them."

That suited me fine, but I didn't say so. Some time in

the future, the near future, I hoped, developments would persuade her to talk about buttons at length, but it would be a mistake to try to crowd her until I knew more. For the sake of appearances I insisted a little, but she didn't listen. I thanked her again for the water and left. As I got the Heron turned around and headed out I was thinking that if I had the equipment in the car, and if it was dark, and if I was willing to risk doing a stretch, I would tap her telephone, quick.

A telephone was what I wanted, quick, and I had noticed one, an outdoor booth, as I had passed a filling station after turning right at the church. Within five minutes after leaving Ellen Tenzer I was in it and was giving the operator a number I didn't have to get from my notebook. It was after eleven, so Wolfe would probably answer it himself.

He did. "Yes?" He has never answered a telephone right and never will.

"Me. From a booth in Mahopac. Has Saul phoned in?"

"No."

"Then he will around noon. I suggest that you send him up here. The niece can wait. The aunt knows who put the overalls on the baby."

"Indeed. She told you so?"

"No. Three points. First, she didn't ask the right questions. Second, she got nervous and bounced me. Third, yesterday's *Times* was there on a table. She doesn't know I saw it. It was folded and there was a bowl of fruit on it, but at the top of the page that showed was a headline that started with the words 'JENSEN REFUSES'. The ad was on that page. So she had seen the ad, but when I dropped in and said I was interested in the horsehair buttons she made she didn't mention it. When she got around to the right question she put it wrong. She asked how I found out she made buttons. She might as well have asked how did Nero Wolfe get results from his ad so soon. Then she realized she wasn't handling it right and bounced me. One will get you twenty that she's not the mother. If she's not sixty she's close. But one will get you forty that she knows what the baby was wearing, that's the least she knows. Am I being impetuous?"

"No. Do you want to turn her over to Saul?"

"I do not. If he could crack her I could. I don't think anybody could until we know more about her. She may be phoning someone right now, but that can't be helped. I'm going back and stake out. If she's phoning, someone may come, or she may go. We can cover her around the clock if you get Fred and Orrie. You'll send Saul?"

"Yes."

"He'll need directions and you need a pencil."

"I have one."

"Okay." I gave the directions, not forgetting to mention the fork. "Three-tenths of a mile from where he hits the gravel there's a wide spot where he can pull off and sit in his car. If I don't show within an hour I'm not around, she has left and so have I, and he'd better go to a phone and call you to see if you've heard from me. He could go to the house first for a look. She might have a visitor and I might have my head stuck in a window trying to hear. Have you any suggestions?"

"No. I'll get Fred and Orrie. When will you eat?"

I told him tomorrow maybe. Returning to the Heron and climbing in, and deciding that as the day wore on it might not be so funny, I headed for Main Street, found a market, and got chocolate bars, bananas, and a carton of milk. I should have told Wolfe I would. He can't stand the notion of a man skipping a meal.

Driving back, I was considering where to leave the car. There were spots not too far from the mailbox where I could ease it in among the trees, but if she went for a ride I would have to get it out to the road in a hurry, and she might go the other way; I didn't know where the gravel road went over the hill. I decided that getting it into the woods far enough to hide it was out, and therefore it might as well be handy. Anyway she had seen it, and if and when it tailed her in broad daylight she would know it. I could only hope she would stay put until Saul came with a car she hadn't seen. I left the Heron in the open, less than a hundred yards from the mailbox, where a gap between trees left enough roadside room, and took to the woods. I am neither an Indian nor a Boy Scout, but if she had been looking out a window I don't think she would have seen me as I made my way to where I had a view of the house from behind a bush. Also a view of the garage.

The garage was empty.

It called for profanity, and I used some, out loud. I don't apologize for either the profanity or the situation I would have done it again in the same circumstances. If we were going to keep her covered I had to leave sooner or later to get to a phone, and right away, while she was looking it over and perhaps making a phone call, and deciding what to do, was not only as good a time as any, it was the best—until the empty garage showed me that it had been the worst.

All right, my luck was out. I dodged through the trees to the clearing, crossed it, went to the door, and banged on it. There might be someone else in the house, though no one had been visible when I was in it. I waited half a minute and banged again, louder, and bellowed, "Anybody home?" After another half a minute I tried the doorknob. Locked. There were two windows to the right, and I went and tried them. Also locked. I went around the corner of the house, taking care not to step in flower beds, which was damn good manners in the circumstances, and there was a window wide open. She had left in a hurry. I didn't have to touch the window. All I had to do was stick a leg in, wiggle my rump onto the sill, and pull the other leg in, and I had broken and entered.

It was a bedroom. I sang out good and loud, "Hey, the house is on fire!" and stood and listened. Not a sound, but to make sure I did a quick tour—two bedrooms, bathroom, living room, and kitchen. Nobody, not even a cat.

She might have merely gone to the drugstore for aspirin and be back any minute. If so, I decided, let her find me in the house. I would tackle her. Almost certainly she was an accessory to something. I don't know all the New York statutes by heart, but there must be a law about leaving babies in people's vestibules, so I wouldn't bother to keep an ear cocked for the sound of a car coming up the hill.

The most likely find was letters or phone numbers, or maybe a diary, and I started in the living room. The *Times* was still on the table under the bowl of fruit. I unfolded it to see if she had clipped the ad; it was intact. There was no desk, but the table had a drawer, and there were three drawers in the stand in a corner that held the telephone. In one of the latter was a card with half a dozen phone numbers, but they were all local. No letters anywhere. There were bookshelves at one wall, some with books and some with magazines and knick-knacks. Going through books takes time, so I left that for the second time around and moved to a bedroom, the one that was obviously hers.

That was where I rang the bell, in the bottom drawer of the bureau. A once-over isn't very thorough and I nearly missed it, but at the bottom, underneath a winter-weight nightgown, there it was—or rather, there they were. Not one, two—two pairs of blue corduroy overalls, each with four white horsehair buttons. The same size as those in the glove compartment of the Heron. A week ago I wouldn't have thought it possible that I would ever get so much pleasure from looking at baby clothes. After gloating a full minute I put them back in the drawer and went and opened a door to a closet. I wanted more.

Eventually I got more, but not in the closet. Not even in the house, strictly speaking, but in the cellar. It was a real cellar, not just a hole for an oil-burning furnace. The space for the furnace was partitioned off, and the rest was what a cellar ought to be, with cupboards and shelves with canned goods. There was even a rack with bottles of wine. Also there were some metal objects propped against the wall in a corner, and I didn't have to assemble them to tell that they were a baby's crib. Also there were three suitcases and two trunks, and one of the trunks contained diapers, rubber pants, bibs, rattles, balloons (not inflated), undershirts, T-shirts, sweaters, and various other garments and miscellaneous items.

With my hankering for baby clothes fully satisfied, and with the house still to myself, I started over again, in the living room. There must be something somewhere that would give a hint on where and who the baby had come from. But there wasn't. I'll skip the next hour and a half, except to say that I know how to look for something that isn't supposed to be found, and I did a job on that house. It takes more time when you leave everything the way it was, but I did a job. All I had when I finished was a few names and addresses, from letters and envelopes in a drawer in the bedroom, and a few phone numbers, and none of them looked promising.

I was hungry, and since I was there uninvited it would have been vulgar to help myself from her kitchen. Also it was twenty minutes to three and Saul had probably come some time ago, so I left, through the window I had entered by, took the driveway to the road and turned right, and when I rounded the bend saw Saul's car, off the road at the wide spot. When he saw me he flopped over on the seat, and when I arrived he was snoring. He isn't much to look at, with his big nose and square chin and wide sloping brow, and snoring with his mouth open he was a sight. I reached in the open window and twisted his nose, and in a millionth of a second he had my wrist and was twisting it. There you are. He knew I would go for his nose before I did.

"Uncle," I said.

He let go and sat up. "What day is it?"

"Christmas. How long have you been here?"

"An hour and twenty minutes."

"Then you should have left twenty minutes ago. Follow instructions."

"I'm a detective. I saw the Heron. Would you care for a sandwich and raisin cake and milk? I've had mine."

"Would I." There was a carton on the back seat and I got in and opened it. Corned beef on rye, two of them. As I unwrapped one I said, "She skipped while I was gone to phone for you. She's been gone over three hours." I took a bite.

"That's life. Anyone else there?"

"No."

"Did you find anything?"

Not had I entered; that was taken for granted. I swallowed and got the carton of milk. "If any of your girl friends has twins there's enough stuff in the cellar, in a trunk, for both of them. And in a drawer upstairs are two pairs of blue corduroy overalls with white horsehair buttons. Of course that's why they're not in the trunk, the buttons. Also in the cellar is the crib the baby slept in."

When I briefed him Thursday evening I had given him the whole picture. With him we nearly always do. He took half a minute to look at this addition to it. "The clothes could be explained," he said, "but the crib settles it."

"Yeah." My mouth was full.

"So the baby was there and she knows the answer. She may not know who the mother is, but she knows enough. How tough is she?"

"She's the kind that might surprise you. I *think* she would clam up. If she came and found me there I was going to tackle her, but now I don't know. Your guess is as good as mine. Probably the best bet is to cover her for at least a couple of days."

"Then we shouldn't be sitting here in my car. She knows your car, doesn't she?"

I nodded and took a swig of milk. "Okay." I put the milk and the rest of the sandwich in the carton. "I'll go and finish this little snack, which is saving my life, in the Heron. Stick your car in the woods and then join me. If she comes before I leave you can duck. I'll go home and report. If he decides on the cover, either Fred or Orrie will be here by nine o'clock. You decide how you want him to make contact and tell me. If he decides he wants her brought in so he can tackle her himself, I'll come instead of Fred or Orrie, and I may need your help."

I climbed out, with the carton. Saul asked, "If she comes before I join you?"

"Stay with your car. I'll find it." I started up the road.

Chapter 6

Saul Panzer and Fred Durkin and Orrie Cather, in
shifts, had Ellen Tenzer's house, or the approach
to it, under surveillance for twenty hours—Saul
from three p.m. to nine p.m. Friday, Fred from nine
p.m. Friday to six a.m. Saturday, and Orrie from six
a.m. to eleven a.m. Saturday. And nobody came.

When Wolfe came down to the office at eleven o'clock
Saturday morning, a glance at my face answered his
question before he asked it. I had no news. In his hand,
as always, were the orchids he had picked for the honor
of a day in the office. He put them in the vase on his
desk, got his bulk adjusted in his chair, and went
through the morning mail which I had opened. Finding
nothing interesting or useful in it, he shoved it aside
and frowned at me.

"Confound it," he growled, "that woman has skedad-
dled. Hasn't she?"

I got a quarter from my pocket, tossed it onto my
desk, and looked at it. "Heads," I said. "No."

"Pfui. I want an opinion."

"You do not. Only a damn fool has an opinion when he
can't back it up, and you know it. You are merely

reminding me that if I had stayed there instead of going to phone you I would have been on her tail."

"That was not in my mind."

"It's in mine. It was just bad luck, sure, but luck beats brains. My getting in the house and finding things doesn't square it. We would only have had to inquire around for an hour or so to learn that she had had a baby there. I hate bad luck. Saul phoned."

"When?"

"Half an hour ago. The niece didn't have a baby in December, January, or February. He has checked on her for that whole period and will report details. He is now finding out if the aunt has been to the niece's apartment since yesterday noon. It's nice to have brains *and* luck. He'll phone around noon to ask if he is to relieve Orrie and—"

The phone rang and I swiveled to get it.

"Nero Wolfe's off—"

"Orrie Cather speaking. A booth in Mahopac."

"Well?"

"No. Not well at all. At ten-fifty-five a car came, state police, and turned in. Three men got out, a trooper, and one I suppose was a county dep, and Purley Stebbins. They went and tried the door and then they went around the corner and the dep climbed in that open window and Stebbins and the trooper went back to the door. Pretty soon it opened and they went in. It didn't look like I could help any so I dusted. Do I go back?"

"How sure are you it was Purley?"

"Nuts. I didn't say I thought it was, I said it was. I'm reporting."

"You certainly are. Come in."

"If I went back maybe I—"

"Damn it, come in!"

I cradled the phone gently, took a breath, and turned. "That was Orrie Cather speaking, a booth in Mahopac. I told him to come in because the aunt won't be coming home. She's dead. Three men came in a state police car and are in the house, and one of them *is* Purley Stebbins. It doesn't take luck *or* brains to know that a New York Homicide sergeant doesn't go to Putnam County looking for white horsehair buttons."

Wolfe's lips were pressed so tight he didn't have any. They parted. "A presumption is not a certainty."

"I can settle *that*." I turned and lifted the phone and dialed the *Gazette* number, and when Wolfe heard me ask for Lon Cohen he pulled his phone over and got on. Lon is on one of his phones at least half of the time and usually you have to wait or leave a message, but I caught him in between and had him right away. I asked him if I still had a credit balance, and he said on poker no, on tips on tidings yes.

"Not much of a tip this time," I told him. "I'm checking on a rumor I just heard. Have you got anything on a woman named Tenzer? Ellen Tenzer?"

"Ellen Tenzer."

"Right."

"We might have. Don't be so damned roundabout, Archie. If you want to know how far we have got on a murder just say so."

"So."

"That's more like it. We haven't got very far unless more has come in the last hour. Around six o'clock this morning a cop glanced in a car, a Rambler sedan, that was parked on Thirty-eighth Street near Third Avenue and saw a woman in the back, on the floor. She had been strangled with a piece of cord that was still around her throat and had been dead five or six hours. She has been tentatively identified as Ellen Tenzer of Mahopac, New York. That's it. I can call downstairs for the latest and call you back if it's that important."

I told him no, thanks, it wasn't important at all, and hung up. So did Wolfe. He glared at me and I glared back.

"This makes it nice," I said. "Talk about ifs."

He shook his head. "Futile."

"One particular if. If I had stuck and gone to work on her then and there I might have opened her up and she would be here right now and we would be wrapping it up. To hell with intelligence guided by experience."

"Futile."

"What isn't, now? We couldn't have asked for anything neater than white horsehair buttons, and now we've got absolutely nothing, and we'll have Stebbins and Cramer on our necks. Thirty-eighth Street is in Homicide South."

"Homicide is their problem, not ours."

"Tell them that. The niece will tell them that a button merchant named Archie Goodwin got her to give him her aunt's address Thursday afternoon. The guy at the filling station will describe the man who wanted directions to her place Friday morning. They'll find thousands of my fingerprints all over the house, including the cellar, nice and fresh. I might as well call Parker now and tell him to get set to arrange bail when I'm booked as a material witness."

Wolfe grunted. "You can supply no information relevant to the murder."

I stared. "The hell I can't."

"I think not. Let's consider it." He leaned back and closed his eyes, but his lips didn't start the in-and-out routine. That was needed only for problems that were really tough. In a minute he opened his eyes and straightened. "It's fairly simple. A woman came with those overalls and hired me to find out where the buttons came from, and I placed that advertisement. It was answered by Beatrice Epps, and she told you of Anne Tenzer, and Anne Tenzer told you of her aunt, and you went to Mahopac. Since the aunt is dead, the rest is entirely at your discretion. You can't be impeached. As a suggestion: she said she was about to leave to keep an appointment, and after a brief conversation you asked permission to wait there until she returned, and she gave it, saying that she didn't know how long it would be. There alone, and curious about the importance of the white horsehair buttons to our client, and having time to pass, you explored the premises. That should do."

"Not naming the client?"

"Certainly not."

"Then it won't be material witness. Withholding evidence. She made the buttons the client wanted to know about, and I was there asking about them, and she got in touch with someone who is connected with the buttons, and the client is connected with the buttons, so they want to ask her questions, so I will name her or else."

"You have a reply. The client had no knowledge of Ellen Tenzer; she hired me to find out where the buttons came from. Therefore it is highly improbable that Ellen Tenzer had knowledge of the client. We are not obliged to disclose a client's name merely because the police would like to test a tenuous assumption."

I took a minute to look at it. "We might get away with it," I conceded. "I can take it if you can. As for your suggestion, you left out my going to phone you and buy lunch, but if they dig that up I can say that was after she left. However, I have a couple of questions. Maybe three. Isn't it likely that Ellen Tenzer would still be alive if you hadn't taken this job and run the ad and sent me to see her?"

"More than likely."

"Then wouldn't the cops be more likely to nail the character who killed her if they know what we know, especially about the baby?"

"Certainly."

"Okay. You said, quote, 'Homicide is their problem, not ours.' If you mean that all the way, it will get on my nerves. It might even cost me some sleep. I saw her and was in her house and spoke with her, and she gave me a drink of water. I'm all for protecting a client's interests, and I'm against Lucy Valdon's being heckled by the cops, and she gave me a martini, but at least she's still alive."

"Archie." He turned a hand over. "My commitment is to learn the identity of the mother and establish it to the client's satisfaction, and to demonstrate the degree of probability that her husband was the father. Do you think I can do that without also learning who killed that woman?"

"No."

"Then don't badger me. It's bad enough without that." He reached to the button to ring for beer.

Chapter 7

I was in custody from 3:42 p.m. Sunday, when Inspector Cramer took me down, to 11:58 a.m. Monday, when Nathaniel Parker, the lawyer Wolfe calls on when only the law will do, arrived at the District Attorney's office with a paper signed by a judge, who had fixed the bail at $20,000. Since the average bail for material witnesses in murder cases in New York is around eight grand, that put me in an upper bracket and I appreciated the compliment.

Except for the loss of sleep and missing two of Fritz's meals and not brushing my teeth, the custody was no great hardship, and no strain at all. My story, following Wolfe's suggestion with a couple of improvements, was first told to Inspector Cramer in the office, with Wolfe present, and after that, with an assistant DA named Mandel whom I had met before, and an assortment of Homicide Bureau dicks, and at one point the DA himself, all I had to do was hold on. The tone had been set by Wolfe, Sunday afternoon in his bout with Cramer, especially at the end, after Cramer had stood up to go.

He had had to tilt his head back, which always peeves him. "I owe you nothing," he had said. "I am not obliged by your forbearance. You know it would be pointless to take me along with Mr. Goodwin, since I would be mute, and the only result would be that if at any time in the future I have a suggestion to offer it would not be offered to you."

"One result," Cramer rasped, "might be that it would be a long time before you could offer any suggestions."

"Pfui. If you really thought that likely you would take me. You have in your pocket a statement signed by me declaring that I have no knowledge whatever, no inkling, of the identity of the murderer of Ellen Tenzer, and I have good ground for my conviction that my client has none. As for your threat to deprive me of my license, I would sleep under a bridge and eat scraps before I would wantonly submit a client to official harassment."

Cramer shook his head. "You eating scraps. Good God. Come on, Goodwin."

We had no inkling of the identity of the mother, either, and had taken no steps to get one, though we hadn't been idle. We had let Saul and Fred and Orrie go. We had read the newspapers. We had sent me to ask Lon Cohen if the *Gazette* had anything that hadn't been printed. We had also sent me to see the client. We had mailed fifty bucks to Beatrice Epps. We had answered phone calls, two of them being from Anne Tenzer and Nicholas Losseff.

I admit that it would have been a waste of the client's money to have Saul and Fred and Orrie check on Ellen Tenzer, since that was being done by city employees and journalists. From the papers and Lon Cohen we had more facts than we could use and more than you would care about. She had been a registered nurse but had quit working at it ten years ago, when her mother had died and she had inherited the house at Mahopac and enough to get by on. She had never married but apparently had liked babies, for she had boarded more than a dozen of them during the ten years, one at a time. Where they had come from and gone to wasn't known; specifically, no one knew anything about her last boarder except that it was a boy, it had been about one month old when it had arrived, in March, she had called it Buster, and it had left about three weeks ago. If anyone had ever visited it nobody had seen him come or go. The best source of information about the babies, the local doctor who had been called on as needed, was a tightlip. Lon doubted if even Purley Stebbins had got anything out of him.

Besides the niece, Anne, the only surviving relatives were a brother and his wife, Anne's parents, who lived in California. Anne was refusing to talk to reporters, but Lon said that apparently she hadn't seen her aunt very often and didn't know much about her.

When I had got up to go Lon had said, "All take and no give, all right, there's still a balance. But I can ask a question. Did you find the buttons? Yes or no."

Having played poker with him a lot of nights, I had had plenty of practice handling my face in his presence. "If you had a trained mind like me," I said, "you wouldn't do that. We ran that ad, and now we want to know about Ellen Tenzer, so you assume there's a connection. None at all. Wolfe likes white horsehair buttons on his pants."

"I raise."

"For his suspenders," I said, and went.

The phone call from Nicholas Losseff came Saturday afternoon. I had been expecting it, since of course Anne Tenzer would have told the cops that Archie Goodwin was from the Exclusive Novelty Button Company, and they would see him, and no one enjoys talking with homicide dicks. So he would be sore. But he wasn't. He only wanted to know if I had found out where the buttons came from. I asked him if he had had official callers, and he said yes, that was why he thought I might have news for him. I told him I was afraid I never would have, and *then* he was sore. If I ever get as hipped on one thing as he was, it won't be buttons.

Anne Tenzer phoned Sunday morning. I was expecting that too, since my name had been in the papers' accounts of the developments in what the *News* called the baby-sitter murder. One paper said I was Nero Wolfe's assistant and another said I was his legman. I don't know which one Anne Tenzer had seen. She *was* sore, but she didn't seem to know exactly why. Not that she resented my pretending to be a button man, and not that she blamed me for what had happened to her aunt. When we hung up I took a minute to consider it and decided that she was sore because she was phoning me. It might give me the false impression that she wanted to hear my voice again. Which it did. Granting it was false, she should have settled on exactly what she was sore about before she dialed.

Nobody is ever as famous as he thinks he is, including me. When, keeping an appointment I had made on the phone, I pushed the button in the vestibule on West Eleventh Street, Sunday morning, and was admitted by Marie Foltz, there was no sign that she had seen my name in the paper. I was just an interruption to what she had been doing. And when I entered the big room one flight up and approached the client, who was at the piano, she finished a run before she turned on the bench and said politely, "Good morning. I suppose you have news?"

My tongue wanted to ask if she had ever finished the martini, but I vetoed it. "Of a sort," I said. "If you have seen the morning paper—"

"I've seen it but I haven't read it. I never do."

"Then I'll have to brief you." I got a chair and moved it up to a polite distance, and sat. "If you never read the papers I suppose you didn't see Mr. Wolfe's ad on Thursday."

"No. An ad?"

"Right. You may remember that I thought the buttons on the overalls were unusual, and he thought so too. The ad offered a reward for information about white horsehair buttons, and we got some. After some maneuvering that wouldn't interest you, I went to Mahopac Friday morning—do you know where Mahopac is?"

"Of course."

"And called on a woman named Ellen Tenzer, having learned that she made white horsehair buttons. We have now learned more about her, not from her. She made the buttons that are on the baby's overalls. And the baby came from her house. It's a small house, no one lived there but her, except the baby. It was there about three months."

"Then she's the mother!"

"No. For various good reasons, no. I won't—"

"But she knows who the mother is!"

"Probably she did. At least she knew where she got it and who from. But she won't tell because she's dead. She was—"

"*Dead?*"

"I'm telling you. After a short talk with her Friday

morning I left to get to a phone and send for help, and
when I got back to the house her car was gone and so
was she. I spent three hours searching the house. I'm
reporting only the details that you need to understand
the situation. Ellen Tenzer never returned to her
house. At six o'clock yesterday morning a cop found a
dead woman in a parked car—here in Manhattan,
Thirty-eighth Street near Third Avenue. She had been
strangled with a piece of cord. It was Ellen Tenzer, and
it was her car. You would know about that if you read
the papers. So she can't tell us anything."

Her eyes were wide. "You mean . . . she was murdered?"

"Right."

"But what— That's terrible."

"Yeah. I'm describing the situation. If the police
don't already know that I was there and combed the
house, including the cellar, they soon will. They'll know
that right after I talked with her she drove away in her
car, and that about fourteen hours later she was murdered. They'll want to know why I went to see her and
what was said. The what was said is no problem, since
we were alone and she's dead, but why I went is harder.
They'll know I went to ask about buttons, but why?
Who was curious enough about buttons to hire Nero
Wolfe? They'll want the client's name, in fact they'll
demand it, and if they get it you will be invited to the
District Attorney's office to answer questions. Then
they'll get theories, and probably one of the theories
will be that the baby wasn't left in your vestibule, that's
just your story to account for having it in your house,
and investigating that theory will be a picnic. Your
friends will get a big kick out of it. The point is—"

"No!"

"No what?"

"I don't— You're going too fast." She was frowning, concentrating. "That's not a *story*. The baby *was* left in my vestibule."

"Sure, but it's not a bad theory. I've known a lot worse. The point is that if we name the client you'll be in for a little trouble, even if they don't happen on that particular theory. And if we refuse—"

"Wait a minute." Her frown was deeper.

I waited more than a minute while she sorted it out. "I guess I'm confused," she said. "Do you mean that woman was murdered on account of—because you went to see her? What you said or something?"

I shook my head. "That's not the way to put it. Put it that she was probably murdered—*very* probably— because someone didn't want her to tell something or do something about the baby that was left in your vestibule. Or put it that if the inquiry about the baby hadn't been started and got to her, she wouldn't have been murdered."

"You're saying that I'm responsible for a murder."

"I am not. That's silly. Whoever put the baby in your vestibule with that note pinned to it must have known you would try to find out where it came from. The responsibility for the murder belongs to him, so don't try to claim it."

"I hate it." She was gripping the edges of the bench. "I *hate* it. Murder. You said I would be *invited* to the District Attorney's office. The questions, the talk—"

"There was an if, Mrs. Valdon. If we name the client. I started to add—"

"Why don't you call me Lucy?"

"Tell me to in writing and I will. You're very giddy for a girl who doesn't know how to flirt. I started to add, if we refuse to name the client *we* may be in trouble, but that's our lookout. We would rather not name you, and we won't, if. If you won't name yourself."

"But I—why should I?"

"You shouldn't, but maybe you have already. Three people know that you have hired Nero Wolfe—your maid, your cook, and your lawyer. Who else?"

"Nobody. I haven't told anyone."

"Are you sure?"

"Yes."

"Well, don't. Absolutely no one. Not even your best friend. People talk, and if talk about your hiring Nero Wolfe gets to the police, that will do it. Lawyers aren't supposed to talk but most of them do, and on him and the maid and cook we'll have to trust to luck. Don't tell them not to, that seldom helps. People are so damn contrary telling them not to mention something gives them the itch. That doesn't apply to you because you have something to lose. Will you bottle it?"

"Yes. But you—what are you going to do?"

"I don't know. Mr. Wolfe has the brains, I only run errands." I stood up. "The immediate problem is keeping you out, that's why I came. They haven't come at us yet, though they found thousands of my prints in that house and as a licensed private detective mine are on file. So they're being cute. For instance, it would have been cute to follow me here. When I left I didn't bother to see if I had a tail; that takes time if he's any good. I walked and made sure of losing him if I had one." I turned, and turned back. "If you think we owe you an apology for letting a mother hunt hatch a murder, here it is."

"I owe *you* an apology." She left the bench. "For

being rude. That day." She took a step. "Are you going?"

"Sure, I've done the errand. And if I had a tail he may be sitting on the stoop waiting to ask me where I've been."

He wasn't. But I had been home less than half an hour when Cramer came and started the wrangle that finally ended at eighteen minutes to four, when he took me.

When I arrived at the old brownstone shortly after noon on Monday, having been bailed out by Parker and given a lift to 35th Street, I was glad to see, as I entered the office, that Wolfe had kept busy during my absence. He had got a good start on another book, *Silent Spring*, by Rachel Carson. I stood until he finished a paragraph, shut the book on a finger, and looked the question.

"Twenty grand," I told him. "The DA wanted fifty, so I'm stepping high. One of the dicks was pretty good, he nearly backed me into a corner on the overalls, but I got loose. No mention of Saul or Fred or Orrie, so they haven't hit on them and now they probably won't. I signed two different statements ten hours apart, but they're welcome to them. The status quo has lost no hide. If there's nothing urgent I'll go up and attend to *my* hide. I had a one-hour nap with a dick standing by. As for eating, what's lunch?"

"Sweetbreads in béchamel sauce with truffles and chervil. Beet and watercress salad. Brie."

"If there's enough you may have some." I headed for the stairs.

I could list five good reasons why I should have quit that job long ago, but I could list six, equally good, why I shouldn't and haven't. Turning it around, I could list two reasons, maybe three, why Wolfe should fire me, and ten why he shouldn't and doesn't. Of the ten, the big one is that if I wasn't around he might be sleeping under a bridge and eating scraps. He hates to work. It has never been said right out, by either of us, that at least half of my salary is for poking him, but it doesn't have to be.

But when I poke hard he is apt to ask if I have any suggestions, and therefore, when we returned to the office after lunch that Monday afternoon and he settled back with his book, I didn't let out a peep. If I had poked and he had asked for suggestions I would have had to pass. I had never seen a dimmer prospect. We had found out where the baby came from, and we were worse off than when we started. Three months had passed since it had arrived at Ellen Tenzer's, so that was hopeless. As for the names and addresses and phone numbers I had collected at the house, I had spent hours on them Saturday afternoon and evening, and none of them was worth a damn, and anyway the cops had them now and they were working on a murder. If anything useful was going to be uncovered by checking on Ellen Tenzer or the baby, the cops would get it. That was probably how Wolfe had it figured as he sat buried in his book. If they tagged the murderer he could go on from there to find the mother. Of course if they tagged someone not only as the murderer but also as the mother, he would have to shave the client's bill, but it would save him a lot of work. I had to admit it would be a waste of Mrs. Valdon's—I mean Lucy's—money to send Saul and Fred and Orrie chasing around Putnam County.

So I didn't poke and he didn't work—anyhow I assumed he didn't. But when he closed the book and put it down at five minutes to four, and pushed his chair back

and rose, to go to the elevator for his afternoon date
with the orchids, he spoke.

"Can Mrs. Valdon be here at six o'clock?"

He must have decided on it hours ago, possibly before lunch, because he doesn't decide things while he's
reading. But he had put off committing himself until the
last minute. Not only would he have to work; he would
have to converse with a woman.

"I can find out," I said.

"Please do so. If not at six, then at nine. Since our
door may be under surveillance, she should enter at the
back." He marched out, and I turned to the phone.

Chapter 8

Entering the old brownstone by the back door is a little more complicated than by the front door, but not much. You come in from 34th Street through a narrow passage between two buildings and end up at a solid wooden gate seven feet high. There is no knob or latch or button to push, and if you have no key for the Hotchkiss lock and haven't been invited you'll need a tool, say a heavy ax. But if you're expected and you knock on the gate it will open, as it did for Lucy Valdon at ten minutes past six that Monday afternoon, and you will be led along a brick walk between rows of herbs, down four steps and on in, and up a stair with twelve steps. At the top, you turn right for the kitchen or left for the office or the front.

I took Lucy to the office. When we entered, Wolfe nodded, barely, tightened his lips, and eyed her with no enthusiasm as she took the red leather chair, put her bag on the stand, and tossed her stole back, sable or something.

"I told Archie I'm sorry I'm a little late," she said. "I didn't realize he would have to wait there for me."

It was a bad start. Since no client has ever called him

Nero or ever will, the "Archie" meant, to him, either
that she was taking liberties or that I already had. He
darted a glance at me, turned to her, and took a breath.
"I don't like this," he said. "This is not a customary
procedure with me, appealing to a client for help. When
I take a job it's *my* job. But I am compelled by circum-
stance. Mr. Goodwin described the situation to you
yesterday morning."

She nodded.

Having settled that point, having got her to acknowledge, by nodding, that my name was Mr. Goodwin, he
leaned back. "But he may not have made the position
sufficiently clear. We're in a pickle. It was obvious that
the simplest way to do the job was to learn where the
baby had come from; once we knew that, the rest would
be easy. Very well, we did that; we know where the
baby came from; and we are stumped. Ellen Tenzer is
dead, and that line of inquiry is completely blocked. You
realize that?"

"Why—yes."

"If you have a reservation about that, dismiss it. To
try to learn how, from where, and by whom the baby
got to Ellen Tenzer would be inept. Such a job is for the
police, with their army of trained men, some of them
competent, and their official standing; not for Mr. Goodwin and me; and presumably they are working at it as
relevant to their investigation of the murder. So for the
present we shall leave Ellen Tenzer to the police, because we must, with this observation: we know that she
didn't put the baby in your vestibule. But we—"

"How do we know that?" Lucy was frowning.

"By inference. She did not attach a piece of paper to a
blanket with a bare pin and wrap the blanket around
the baby. Mr. Goodwin found a tray half full of safety

pins in her house. But he found no rubber-stamp kit and no stamp pad, and one was used for the message on the paper. The inference is not conclusive, but it is valid. I am satisfied that on May twentieth Ellen Tenzer delivered the baby to someone, either at her house or, more likely, at a rendezvous elsewhere. She may or may not have known that its destination was your vestibule. I doubt it; but she knew too much about its history, its origin, so she was killed."

"Then you know that?" Lucy's hands were clasped, the fingers twisted. "That that's why she was killed?"

"No. But it would be vacuous not to assume it. Another assumption: Ellen Tenzer not only did not leave the baby in your vestibule or know that was its destination; she didn't even know that it was to be so disposed of that its source would be unknown and undiscoverable. For if she had known that, she would not have dressed it in those overalls. She knew those buttons were unique and that inquiry might trace their origin. Whatever she—"

"Wait a minute." Lucy was frowning, concentrating. Wolfe waited. In a moment she went on. "Maybe she *wanted* them to be traced."

Wolfe shook his head. "No. In that case her reception of Mr. Goodwin, when she found that they had been traced, would have been quite different. No. Whatever she knew of the baby's past, she knew nothing of its intended future. And whoever left it in your vestibule must have satisfied himself that none of its garments held any clue to its origin, so he didn't know enough about infants' clothing to realize that the buttons were unusual, even extraordinary, and might be traced. But Mr. Goodwin realized it, and so did I."

"I didn't."

He glared at her. "That is informative merely about you, madam, not about the problem. My concern is the problem, and now I not only have to do a job I have undertaken, I must also avoid being charged, along with Mr. Goodwin, with commission of a felony. If Ellen Tenzer was killed to prevent her from revealing facts about the baby that was left in your vestibule, and almost certainly she was, Mr. Goodwin and I are both withholding evidence regarding a homicide, and as I said, we're in a pickle. I do not want to give the police your name and the information you have entrusted to me in confidence. You would be disturbed and pestered, and probably badgered, and you are my client; so my self-esteem would suffer. It is my conceit to expose myself to reproach only from others, never from myself. But if Mr. Goodwin and I withhold your name and what you have told us, it won't do merely to meet our commitment to you and leave the homicide to the police; in addition to finding the mother, we must either also find the murderer or establish that there was no connection between Ellen Tenzer's death and her association with the baby that was left in your vestibule. Since it's highly probable that there was a connection, I shall be tracking a murderer on your behalf and at your expense. Is that clear?"

Lucy's eyes came to me. "I told you I *hate* it."

I nodded. "The trouble is, you can't just bow out. If you drop it, if you're no longer his client, we'll have to open up, at least I will. I'm a VIP, I'm the one who last saw Ellen Tenzer alive. Then you'll have the cops. Now you have us. You'll just have to take your pick, Mrs. Valdon."

She opened her mouth and closed it again. She turned, got her bag from the stand, opened it, took out a slip of paper, rose, stepped to me, and handed me the paper. I took it and read, handwritten in ink:

Monday
To Archie Goodwin—
Call me Lucy.
Lucy Valdon

Picture it. In Wolfe's office, in his presence, his client hands me a note which she must know I would prefer not to show him. It took handling. I raised one brow high, which always annoys him because he can't do it, put the paper in my pocket, and cocked my head at her, back in the red leather chair. "Not if you're no longer a client," I told her.

"But I am. I hate it, the way it is now, but of course I am."

I looked at Wolfe and met his eye. "Mrs. Valdon prefers us to the cops. Good for our self-esteem."

She spoke, to him. "It was the way you said it, tracking a murderer on my behalf. Do you mean—must you do that first?"

"No," he snapped. She was not only a woman, she was a creature who had passed me a private note before his eyes. "That will be incidental but it must be done. So I proceed?"

"Yes."

"Then you'll have to help. For the present we leave Ellen Tenzer to the police and start at the other end— the birth of the baby, and its conception. On Tuesday you gave Mr. Goodwin, with reluctance, the names of four women. We must have more. We want the names of all women who were or might have been in contact

with your husband, however briefly, in the spring of
last year. All of them."

"But that's impossible. I couldn't name all of them."
She gestured with the wedding-ring hand. "My husband met hundreds of people that I didn't meet—for
instance, I almost never went to literary cocktail parties with him. They bored me, and anyway he had a
better time if I wasn't there."

Wolfe grunted. "No doubt. You will give Mr. Goodwin all the names you do know, reserving none. Their
owners will not suffer any annoyance, since inquiry
about them can be restricted to one point, their whereabouts at the time the baby was born. It is an advantage
that a woman can't carry a baby, and bear it, without
interruption of her routine. Very few of them will have
to be approached directly, possibly none. You will omit
no one."

"All right. I won't."

"You also gave Mr. Goodwin some names of men, and
we shall now make use of them, at least some, but for
that we need your help. We can start with only a few of
them, say three or four, and go on to others if we must.
I shall want to see them, and they will come here, since
I never leave my house on business. I need not see them
separately; in a group will do. You will arrange that,
after they have been selected."

"You mean I'll ask them to come to see you?"

"Yes."

"But what will I tell them?"

"That you have hired me to make an investigation for
you, and I wish to talk with them."

"But then . . ." She was frowning. "Archie told me
to tell no one, not even my best friend."

"Mr. Goodwin was following instructions. On further

consideration I have concluded that the risk must be
taken. You say that your husband knew hundreds of
people you have never met. I trust that the 'hundreds'
was an overestimate, but if there are dozens I must
have every name. You say you hate it the way it is now.
Confound it, madam, so do I. If I had known the job
would develop thus—a murder, and my involvement,
and routine fishing in a boundless sea—I wouldn't have
taken it. I must see the three or four men who are best
qualified to complete the list of your husband's acquain-
tances, and to give me information about him which you
do not have. After you and Mr. Goodwin select them,
will you get them here?"

She was hating it even more. "What do I say when
they ask what you're investigating for me?"

"Say I'll explain to them. Of course that will be tick-
lish. Certainly there will be no mention by me of the
baby left in your vestibule with that message. That
there is a baby in your house is probably more widely
known than you suspect, but if one or more of them asks
about it I shall say that is immaterial. When I decide
precisely what I'll tell them you will be informed, before I see them, and if you have objections they will be
considered." He swiveled to look at the clock. Half an
hour till dinner. He swiveled back. "You and Mr. Goodwin will decide this evening on the three or four men to
be chosen from among your husband's familiars. I
would like to see them either at eleven tomorrow morning or at nine tomorrow evening. You will also compile
the list of women's names. But one question now: will
you please tell me where you were last Friday evening?
From eight o'clock on?"

Her eyes widened. "Friday?"

He nodded. "I have no ground whatever, madam, to

doubt your good faith. But I now have to deal with someone who doesn't flinch from murder, and it isn't wholly inconceivable that you are a Jezebel. Ellen Tenzer was killed Friday around midnight. Where were you?"

Lucy stared. "But you don't . . . you couldn't think . . ."

"Wildly improbable but conceivable. You should be gratified that I consider it imaginable that you have gulled me by a superb display of wile and guile."

She tried to smile. "You have a strange idea of what gratifies people." She looked at me. "Why didn't you ask me this yesterday?"

"I meant to but forgot."

"Do you mean that?"

"No, but he's right, it's a compliment. Think how good you would have to be to make monkeys of him *and* me. Where were you Friday night?"

"All right. Friday." She took a moment. "I went out for dinner, to a friend's apartment, Lena Guthrie, but I got home in time for the ten-o'clock feeding—the baby. The nurse was there, but I usually like to be there too. Then I went downstairs and played the piano awhile, and then I went to bed." She turned to Wolfe. "This is absolute nonsense!"

"No," he growled. "Nothing is nonsense that is concerned with the vagaries of human conduct. If the nurse is there this evening, Mr. Goodwin will ask her about Friday."

Chapter 9

There were three men with us in the office at noon the next day, Tuesday, but they were not ex-familiars of the late Richard Valdon. Saul Panzer was in the red leather chair. On two of the yellow chairs fronting Wolfe's desk were Fred Durkin, five feet ten, 190 pounds, bald and burly, and Orrie Cather, six feet flat, 180 pounds, good design from tip to toe. Each had in his hand some three-by-five cards on which I had typed information which had been furnished by the client, and in his wallet some used fives and tens which I had got from the drawer in the safe.

Wolfe's eyes were at Fred and Orrie, as always when briefing that trio. He knew Saul was getting it. "There should be no difficulties or complications," he said. "It's quite simple. Early this year, or possibly late last year, a woman gave birth to a baby. I want to find her. But your present mission is restricted to elimination. Regarding each of the women whose names are on those cards, you are merely to answer the question, could she have borne a baby at that time? When you find one who is not easily eliminated, whose whereabouts and movements during that period need more elaborate inquiry, go no further without consulting me. Is that clear?"

"Not very," Orrie said. "How easy is 'easily'?"

"That's inherent in the approach I suggest, devised by Archie and me. You will address the woman herself only if you must. In most cases, perhaps all, you can get enough information from others—apartment-house staffs, tradesmen, mailmen—you know the routines. You will use your own names, and your inquiries are on behalf of the Dolphin Corporation, owner and operator of Dolphin Cottages, Clearwater, Florida. A woman is suing the corporation for a large sum in damages, half a million dollars, for injuries she suffered on Saturday, January sixth, this year, as she was stepping from a dock into a boat. She claims that the employee of the corporation who was handling the boat allowed it to move and her injuries resulted from his negligence. The case will come to trial soon, and the corporation wants the testimony of one Jane Doe (a name from one of your cards). Jane Doe was a tenant of one of the corporation's cottages from December tenth to February tenth; she was on the dock when the incident occurred, and she told the manager of the cottages that the boat did not move and the boatman was not at fault. Am I too circumstantial?"

"No," Fred said. Whether he knew what 'circumstantial' meant or not, he thought Wolfe couldn't be too anything.

"The rest is obvious. There is no Jane Doe, and never has been, at the address the Dolphin Corporation has for her, and you are trying to find her. Could she be the Jane Doe on your card? Was she in Florida from December tenth to February tenth? No? Where was she?" Wolfe flipped a hand. "But you need no suggestions on how to make sure. You will be merely eliminating. Is it clear?"

"Not to me." Orrie looked up from his notebook, in which he had been scribbling. "If the only question is did she have a baby, why drag in Florida and dolphins and a lawsuit?" His bumptious tone came from his belief that all men are created equal, especially him and Nero Wolfe.

Wolfe's head turned. "Answer him, Saul."

Saul's notebook was back in his pocket, with the cards. He looked at Orrie as at an equal, which he wasn't. "Evidently," he said, "the chances are that the baby was a bastard and she went away to have it, so was she away? And if she wasn't, the one thing that anybody would know about what a woman was doing five months ago is that she was having a baby, or wasn't. The Florida thing is just to get started."

That wasn't fair, Wolfe's part in it, since Saul had been given the whole picture five days ago, but the idea was to teach Orrie better manners, and of course Saul had to play up. When they had gone and I returned to the office after seeing them out, I told Wolfe, "You know, if you pile it on enough to give Orrie an inferiority complex it will be a lulu, and a damn good op will be ruined."

He snorted. "Pfui. Not conceivable." He picked up *Silent Spring* and got comfortable. Then his chin jerked up and he said politely. "You're aware that I'm not going to ask you what was on that paper that woman handed you yesterday."

I nodded. "It had to be mentioned sooner or later. If it had anything to do with my job, naturally I'd report it. I will anyway. It said in longhand: 'Dearest Archie,

Lizzie Borden took an ax, and gave her mother forty whacks. Your loving Lucy.' In case you wonder—"

"Shut up." He opened the book.

We still didn't know how many would come to the stag party that evening, and it was late afternoon when Lucy phoned that she had booked all four of them. When Wolfe came down from the plant rooms at six o'clock the notes I had typed were on his desk. As follows:

MANUEL UPTON. In his fifties. Editor of *Distaff*, the "magazine for any and every woman," circulation over eight million. He had started Richard Valdon on the road to fame and fortune ten years back by publishing several of his short stories, and had serialized two of his novels. Married, wife living, three grown children. Home, a Park Avenue apartment.

JULIAN HAFT. Around fifty. President of the Parthenon Press, publisher of Valdon's novels. He and Valdon had been close personally for the last five years of Valdon's life. Widower, two grown children. Home, a suite in Churchill Towers.

LEO BINGHAM. Around forty. Television producer. No business relations with Valdon, but had been his oldest and closest friend. Bachelor. Gay-dog type. Home, a penthouse on East 38th Street.

WILLIS KRUG. Also around forty. Literary agent. Valdon had been one of his clients for seven years. Documentary widower; married and divorced. No children. Home, an apartment on Perry Street in the Village.

Whenever an assortment of guests is expected after dinner, Wolfe, on leaving the table, doesn't return to the office and his favorite chair. He goes to the kitchen, where there is a chair without arms that will take his seventh of a ton with only a little overlap at the edges.

The only time he has been overruled about the furniture in his house was when he bought a king-size armchair for the kitchen and Fritz vetoed it. It was delivered, and he sat in it for half an hour one morning discussing turnip soup with Fritz, but when he came down from the plant rooms at six o'clock it was gone. If he or Fritz ever mentioned it again they did so in privacy.

Since none of the four invited guests could be the mother we were looking for, and there was no reason to suppose that one of them was the murderer, I sized them up only from force of habit as I answered the doorbell and admitted them. Willis Krug, the literary agent, who arrived first, a little early, was a tall bony guy with a long head and flat ears. He started for the red leather chair, but I headed him off because I had decided Bingham should have it—Valdon's oldest and closest friend—and he was the next to show, on the dot at nine o'clock. Leo Bingham, the television producer. He was tall and broad and handsome, with a big smile that went on and off like a neon sign. Julian Haft, the publisher, who came next, was a barrel from the hips up and a pair of toothpicks from the hips down, bald on top, with balloon-tired cheaters. Manuel Upton, editor of *Distaff*, was last to arrive, and looking at him I was surprised that he had arrived at all. A shrimp to begin with, he was sad-eyed and wrinkled, he sagged, and he was panting from climbing the stoop. I was sorry I hadn't saved the red leather chair for him. When he was safe if not sound on one of the yellow ones I went to my desk and buzzed the kitchen on the house phone.

Wolfe entered. Three of the guests rose. Manuel Upton, who had the least to lift, didn't. Wolfe, no handshaker, asked them to sit, went to his desk, and stood while I pronounced names, giving them all-out nods, at least half an inch. He sat, sent his eyes from right to left and back again, and spoke. "I don't thank you for coming, gentlemen, since you are obliging Mrs. Valdon, not me. But I'm appreciative. You're busy men with a day's work behind you. Will you have refreshment? None is before you because that restricts choices, but a supply is at hand. Will you have something?"

Willis Krug shook his head. Julian Haft declined with thanks. Leo Bingham said brandy. Manuel Upton said a glass of water, no ice. I said scotch and water. Wolfe had pushed a button and Fritz was there and was given the order, including beer for Wolfe.

Bingham gave Wolfe the big smile. "I was glad to come. Glad of the chance to meet you." His baritone went fine with the smile. "I've often thought of your enormous possibilities for television, and now that I've seen you and heard your voice—my God, it would be stupendous! I'll come and tell you about it."

Manuel Upton shook his head, slow to the left and slow to the right. "Mr. Wolfe may not understand you, Leo. 'Enormous.' 'Stupendous.'" His croak went fine with all of him. "He may think that's a personal reference."

"Don't you two get started now," Willis Krug said. "You ought to hire the Garden and slug it out."

"We're incompatible," Bingham said. "All magazine men hate television because it's taking all their gravy. In another ten years there won't be any magazines but one. *TV Guide*. Actually I love you, Manny. Thank God you'll have Social Security."

Julian Haft spoke to Wolfe. "This is the way it goes, Mr. Wolfe. Mass culture." His thin tenor went all right with his legs but not with his barrel. "I understand you're a great reader. Thank heaven books don't depend on advertising. Have you ever written one? You should. It might not be enormous or stupendous, but it certainly would be readable, and I would like very much to publish it. If Mr. Bingham can solicit, so can I."

Wolfe grunted. "Unthinkable, Mr. Haft. Maintaining integrity as a private detective is difficult; to preserve it for the hundred thousand words of a book would be impossible for me, as it has been for so many others. Nothing corrupts a man so deeply as writing a book; the myriad temptations are overpowering. I wouldn't presume—"

Fritz had entered with a tray. First the beer to Wolfe, then the brandy to Bingham, the water to Upton, and the scotch and water to me. Upton got a pillbox from a pocket, fished one out and popped it into his mouth, and drank water. Bingham took a sip of brandy, looked surprised, took another sip, rolled it around in his mouth, looked astonished, swallowed, said, "May I?" and got up and went to Wolfe's desk for a look at the label on the bottle. "Never heard of it," he told Wolfe, "and I thought I knew cognac. Incredible, serving it offhand to a stranger. Where in God's name did you get it?"

"From a man I did a job for. In my house a guest is a guest, stranger or not. Don't stint yourself; I have nearly three cases." Wolfe drank beer, licked his lips, and settled back. "As I said, gentlemen, I appreciate your coming, and I won't detain you beyond reason. My client, Mrs. Valdon, said she would leave it to me to explain what she has hired me to do, and I shall be as brief as possible. First, though, it should be understood that everything said here, either by you or by me, is in the strictest confidence. Is that agreed?"

They all said yes.

"Very well. My reserve is professional and merely my obligation to my client; yours will be personal, on behalf of a friend. This is the situation. In the past month Mrs. Valdon has received three anonymous letters. They are in my safe. I'm not going to show them to you or disclose their contents, but they make certain allegations regarding her late husband, Richard Valdon, and they make specific demands. The handwriting, in ink, is obviously disguised, but the sex of the writer is not in question. The contents of the letters make it clear that they were written by a woman. My engagement with Mrs. Valdon is to identify her, speak with her, and deal with her demands."

He reached for his glass, took a swallow of beer, and leaned back. "It's an attempt to blackmail, but if the allegations are true Mrs. Valdon will be inclined to accede to the demands, with qualifications. When I find the letter-writer she will not be exposed or indicted, or compelled to forgo her demands, unless the allegations are false. The first necessity is to find her, and that's the difficulty. Her arrangement for having the demands met is extraordinarily ingenious; nothing so crude as leaving a packet of bills somewhere. I'll suggest its nature. You are men of affairs. Mr. Haft, what if you were told, anonymously, under threat of disclosure of a secret you wished to preserve, to deposit a sum of money to the credit of an account, identified only by number, in a bank in Switzerland? What would you do?"

"Good lord, I don't know," Haft said.

Krug said, "Swiss banks have some funny rules."

Wolfe nodded. "The letter-writer's arrangement is even more adroit. Not only is there no risk of contact, there is no possible line of approach. But she must be found, and I have considered two procedures. One would be extremely expensive and might take many months. The other would require the cooperation of men who were close friends or associates of Mr. Valdon. From Mrs. Valdon's suggestions four names were selected: yours. On her behalf I ask each of you to make a list of the names of all women with whom, to your knowledge, Richard Valdon was in contact during the months of March, April, and May, nineteen-sixty-one. Last year. *All* women, however brief the contact and regardless of its nature. May I have it soon? Say by tomorrow evening?"

Three of them spoke at once, but Leo Bingham's baritone smothered the others. "That's a big order," he said. "Dick Valdon got around."

"Not only that," Julian Haft said, "but there's the question, what's the procedure? There are eight or nine girls and women in my office Dick had *some* contact with. What are you going to do with the names we list?"

"There are four in my office," Willis Krug said.

"Look," Manuel Upton croaked. "You'll have to tell us about the allegations."

Wolfe was drinking beer. He put the empty glass down. "To serve the purpose," he said, "the lists must be all-inclusive. They will be used with discretion. No one will be pestered; no offense will be given; no rumors will be started; no prying curiosity will be aroused. Very few of the owners of the names will be addressed at all. Inferences I have drawn from indications in the letters limit the range of possibilities. You have my firm assurance that you will have no cause for regret that you have done this favor for Mrs. Valdon, with this single qualification: if it should transpire that the writer of the letters is one for whom you have regard, she will of course be vexed and possibly frustrated. That will be your only risk. Have some brandy, Mr. Bingham."

Bingham rose and went for the bottle. "Payola." He poured. "It's a bribe." He took a sip. "But what a bribe!" The big smile.

"I want to hear about the allegations," Upton croaked.

Wolfe shook his head. "That would violate a firm assurance I have given my client. Not discussible."

"She's my client too," Krug said. "I was Dick's agent, and now I'm hers since she owns the copyrights. Also I'm her friend, and I'm against anyone who sends anonymous letters, no matter who. I'll get the list to you tomorrow."

"Hell, I'm hooked," Leo Bingham said. He was standing, twirling the cognac in the snifter. "I've been bribed." He turned to Wolfe. "How about a deal? If you get her from my list I get a bottle of this."

"No, sir. Not by engagement. As a gesture of appreciation perhaps."

Julian Haft had removed his balloon-tired cheaters and was fingering the bows. "The letters," he said. "Were they mailed in New York? The city?"

"Yes, sir."

"Then you have the envelopes?"

"Yes, sir."

"May we see them—just the envelopes? You say the writing is disguised, but it might—one of us might get a hint from it."

Wolfe nodded. "Therefore it would be ill-advised to show them to you. One of you might indeed get a hint of the identity of the writer but not divulge it, and that might complicate the problem for me."

"I have a question," Manuel Upton croaked. "I've heard that there's a baby in Mrs. Valdon's house, and a nurse for it. I know nothing about it, but the person who told me isn't a windbag. Is there any connection between the baby and the letters?"

Wolfe was frowning at him. "A baby? Mrs. Valdon's baby?"

"I didn't say her baby. I said there's a baby in her house."

"Indeed. I'll ask her, Mr. Upton. If it is somehow connected with the letters she must be aware of it. By the way, I have advised her to mention the letters to no one. No exceptions. As you gentlemen know, she didn't mention them to you. The matter is in my hands."

"All right, handle it." Upton got to his feet. His weight was just about half of Wolfe's, but from the effort it took to get it up from a chair it might have been the other way around. "From the way you're handling us, or trying to, you'll hash it up. I don't owe Lucy Valdon anything. If she wants a favor from me she can ask me."

He headed for the door, jostling Leo Bingham's elbow as he passed, and Bingham's other hand darted out and gave him a shove. Because a guest is a guest, and also because I doubted if he had the vim and vigor to shut the door, I got up and went, passed him in the hall, and saw him out. When I returned to the office Julian Haft was speaking.

". . . but before I do so I want to speak with Mrs. Valdon. I don't agree with Mr. Upton, I don't say you're handling it badly, but what you ask is rather—uh—unusual." He put the cheaters back on and turned. "Of course I agree with you, Willis, about people who send anonymous letters. I suppose you think I'm being over-cautious."

"That's your privilege," Krug said.

"To hell with privilege," Bingham said. He flashed the big smile at Haft. "I wouldn't say overcautious, I'd say cagey. You were born scared, Julian."

You have to make allowances. Buyers and sellers. To a literary agent a publisher is a customer, but to a television producer he's just another peddler.

Chapter 10

I have before me a copy of the expense account of the case in the files under V for Valdon. Its second stage, working on the names on the lists furnished by Willis Krug, Leo Bingham, Julian Haft, and the client (we never got one from Manuel Upton) lasted twenty-six days, from June 12 to July 7, and cost the client $8,674.30, not including any part of my salary, which is covered by the fee and is never itemized.

Lucy's list had 47 names, Haft's 81, Bingham's 106, and Krug's 55. One of Upton's daughters, married, was on Haft's and Bingham's lists, but not on Krug's. Haft's married daughter was on Lucy's list but none of the others. A certain friend of Bingham's was on nobody's list; Orrie picked up her name along the way. Of course there were many duplications on the four lists, but there were 148 different names, as follows:

Section	Number	Status
A	57	Single
B	52	Married, living with husbands

C	18	Divorced
D	11	Widowed
E	10	Married, separated

Another statistic, those in each section who had babies between December 1, 1961, and February 28, 1962:

Section	Number
A	1
B	2
C	0
D	1
E	0

The one in Section A (single) who had a baby worked in Krug's office, but everybody knew about it and the baby had been legally given (or sold) to an adoption service. It took Saul nearly two weeks to cinch it that the baby had not got sidetracked somehow and ended up in Mrs. Valdon's vestibule. The one in Section D (widowed) may have been a problem for her friends and enemies, but not for us. Her husband had died two years before the baby came, but she was keeping it and didn't care who knew it. I saw it.

The two babies in Section B (married, living with husbands) were really three; one was twins. They were all living with their parents. Fred saw the twins and Orrie saw the single.

Besides the mothers, two girls in Section A, two women in B, two in C, and one in D, had been away from their homes and/or jobs for a part or all of the period. Orrie had to take a plane to France, the Riviera, to settle one of them, and Fred had to fly to Arizona to settle another one.

There has never been a smoother operation since Whosis scattered the dust on the temple floor. Absolutely flawless. Orrie got taken to an apartment-house superintendent by a doorman, but it wasn't his fault, and Fred got bounced from backstage in a theater, but a bounce is all in the day's work. As an example of superlative snoopery it was a perfect performance. And when Saul phoned at half past three Saturday afternoon, July 7, to report that he had closed the last little gap in the adoption and had actually seen the baby, and the operation was complete, we were precisely where we had been on June 12, twenty-six days earlier.

With a difference, though. There had been a couple of developments, but we hadn't done the developing. One, the minor one, was that I was no longer the last person known to have seen Ellen Tenzer alive. That Friday afternoon she had called at the home of a Mrs. James R. Nesbitt on East 68th Street, an ex-patient from her New York nursing days. Mrs. Nesbitt had waited nearly two weeks to mention it because she didn't want her name to appear in connection with a murder, but had finally decided she must. Presumably the DA had promised her that her name would not appear, but some journalist had somehow got it, and hooray for freedom of the press. Not that Mrs. Nesbitt was really any help. Ellen Tenzer had merely said she needed advice about something from a lawyer and had asked Mrs. Nesbitt to tell her the name of one who could be trusted, and she had done so and had phoned the lawyer to make an appointment. But Ellen Tenzer hadn't kept the appointment. She hadn't told Mrs. Nesbitt why she needed a lawyer. Mrs. Nesbitt was added to Saul's list of names, just in case, but she hadn't had a baby for ten years and her twenty-year-old daughter had never had one.

The other development, the major one, was that the client came within an ace of quitting. She phoned at a quarter after four on Monday, July 2. Of course I had kept in touch with her; when you're spending more than three Cs a day of a client's money and getting nothing for it, the least you can do is give her a ring, or drop in and say hello, it's a fine day but I guess they need rain in the country. I had watched her feed the baby once, lunched with her once, dined with her twice, taught her to play pinochle, and listened to her playing the piano for a total of about six hours. Also we had done a little dancing, to records in the dining room, which wasn't carpeted. She was plenty good enough to spend an evening with at the Flamingo or Gillotti's, but that would have to wait, since it would have broken security. If you ask, would I have gone to so much trouble to keep a client patient if she had been cross-eyed or fat-ankled? the answer is no.

When I answered the phone at a quarter after four on July 2 and started the formula, "Nero Wolfe's—" she broke in, "Can you come, Archie? Right away?"

"I could, sure. Why?"

"A man was here, a policeman. He just left. He asked when I hired Nero Wolfe, and he asked about the baby. Will you come?"

"What did you tell him?"

"Nothing, of course. I said he had no right to ask about my private affairs. That's what you told me to say."

"Right. Did you get his name?"

"He told me, but I was so—I don't know."

"Was it Cramer?"

"Cramer . . . no."

"Rowcliff?"

"No."

"Stebbins?"

"That sounds like it. Stebbins. Yes, I think so."

"Big and solid with a broad nose and a wide mouth and trying hard to be polite?"

"Yes."

"Okay. My favorite cop. At ease. Play the piano. I can do it in twenty minutes since I won't have to bother about a tail."

"You're coming?"

"Certainly."

I hung up, got the house phone, buzzed the plant rooms, and after a wait had Wolfe's voice: "Yes?"

"Mrs. Valdon phoned. Purley Stebbins came and asked her about you *and* the baby. She told him nothing. She wants me to come and I'm leaving. Any instructions?"

"No. Confound it."

"Yes, sir. Bring her?"

"Not unless you must." He hung up.

I went to the kitchen to tell Fritz the phone and the door were his until he saw me again, and was off. As I descended the stoop to the sidewalk and turned east I automatically glanced around, but actually I didn't give a damn, now, if I had a shadow or not. Almost certainly there was an eye on the Valdon house anyway.

I walked it. The five minutes a hack might have saved didn't matter, and my legs like to feel that they're helping out. When I turned into Eleventh Street and neared the house, again I glanced around automatically, but again it didn't matter. The fat was in the fire, and the problem was dodging the spatters. I mounted the four steps to the vestibule, but didn't have to push the button, because the door was standing open and Lucy herself was there. She didn't speak. When I had crossed the sill she closed the door, turned, and made for the stairs. I followed. Apparently she had forgotten the progress we had made in cordial relations. One flight up she entered the big room, shut the door when I was in, faced me, and said, "He asked me if I knew Ellen Tenzer."

"Sure. Naturally."

"You stand there and say *naturally!* I should never—if I hadn't gone to Nero Wolfe—you know that, Archie!"

"Call me Mr. Goodwin."

Her big gray eyes widened.

"The point is," I said, "that mixing personal relations and business relations is bad for both. If you want to hold hands, fine. If you want to be a huffy client, okay. But it's not fair for a huffy client to call me Archie."

"I'm not huffy!"

"All right, crabby."

"I'm not crabby. You know it's true, if I hadn't gone to Nero Wolfe and you hadn't found that woman she wouldn't have been murdered. I *hate* it! And now they know about Nero Wolfe and they know about the baby. I'm going to tell them everything. That's why I asked you to come—to tell me where I go and who I tell. The District Attorney? And I wanted to ask you—will you go with me?"

"No. May I use your phone?"

"Why, yes, if— What for?"

"To tell Mr. Wolfe he's fired, so he can—"

"I didn't say he's fired!"

I raised the brows. "You're rattled, Mrs. Valdon.

We've discussed this several times, what would happen if they got to you and came at you. The understanding was that we would hang on unless it got too hot to handle, and you would let us decide if and when it did. You wanted me to explain the rules, about withholding evidence and obstructing justice and so on, and I did so. It was clearly understood that if and when it was decided to let go, Mr. Wolfe would do it. Now you have decided to let go, so I'll phone him and tell him to go ahead. As for your firing him, call it something else if you prefer—that you're releasing him from his commitment. It does sound better. I'll use the phone downstairs." I turned.

Fingers gripped my arm. "Archie."

I turned back. "Listen," I said, "I'm not putting on an act. But I'll be damned if I'm going to squat and take your shoes off and rub your cold feet."

Her arms went around my neck and she was against me.

So fifteen minutes later, or maybe twenty, we were seated on the couch with martinis and she was saying, "What you said about mixing personal relations and business relations, you know that's silly. We've been doing it for nearly a month, and here we are. I started the first time you were here, exchanging sips with you and telling you I wasn't trying to flirt with you. Why didn't you laugh at me?"

"I did. I told you oysters flirt and you walked out."

She smiled. "I'm going to admit something."

"Good. We'll take turns."

"When I said that, I *honestly* thought I wasn't trying to flirt with you. How can you stand a woman as stupid as that?"

"I can't. I couldn't."

"What?" She frowned. "Oh. Thank you very much, but I am. When you were talking about phoning Nero Wolfe, of course I should have been thinking about what was going to happen, whether I should ask you not to, what I was going to do—all that—but I *was* thinking he'll never kiss me again. I've always known I'm not very smart. For instance, when you asked me just now if that man gave me any hint how he found out I had hired Nero Wolfe—if I had been smart I would have got a hint out of him. Wouldn't I?"

"No. Not out of Purley Stebbins. Sometimes he has trouble deciding what to say next, but he always knows what not to say." I took a sip. "Since we're back on business, let's get it clear. I may be under a false impression. Are you still a client?"

"Yes."

"You're absolutely sure you want to stick it out?"

"Here." She put a hand out and I took it. That was how our cordial relations had started, three weeks back, when I had spent a long evening with her, making up her list and picking the four men to be asked to help. When a handshake goes beyond routine even one second, it's a test. If you both decide it's enough at the same instant, fine. But if she's through before you are, or vice versa, look out. You don't fit. Lucy and I had been simultaneous the first time. We were this time too.

"Okay," I said. "It's quite a limb we're out on. I don't have to describe it, you know it as well as I do. Your part may be tough, but it's simple. You simply say nothing and answer no questions whatever, no matter who asks them. Right?"

"Right."

"If you are invited to call at the District Attorney's

office, decline the invitation. If Stebbins or someone else calls here, see him or not as you please, but tell him nothing, and do *not* try to drag hints out of him. As for how they got onto your hiring Nero Wolfe, and the baby, it doesn't matter how. My guess would be Manuel Upton, but I wouldn't give a nickel to know. If it was Upton, some of the questions you won't answer may be about the anonymous letters. They could turn out to be the toughest item for Mr. Wolfe and me, but we knew that. He told four men they were in his safe. If a court orders him to produce them and he says they never existed, we could be charged with destroying evidence, which is worse than withholding evidence. That would be very funny and I must remember to laugh."

"Archie."

"Yes?"

"Just six weeks ago I was just going along. There was no baby upstairs, I had never seen you, I wouldn't have dreamed it would ever be . . . like this. When I say I hate it you understand, don't you?"

"Sure I do." I glanced at my watch, finished the martini, put the glass down, and rose. "I'd better mosey."

"Must you? Why not stay for dinner?"

"I don't dare. It's half past five. It's even money that either Stebbins or Inspector Cramer will turn up at six or soon after, and I should be there."

She pulled her shoulders in, released them, and left the couch. "And all I have to do is say nothing." She stood, her head tilted up. "Then come back later and tell me. Business relations."

I don't know what it was, what she said or the way she said it or something in her eyes. Whatever it was, I smiled and then I laughed, and then she was laughing too. Half an hour earlier it wouldn't have been reasonable to suppose that we would so soon be having a good laugh together. Obviously it was a good way to end a conversation, so I turned and went.

It was two minutes short of six o'clock when I used my key on the door of the old brownstone, went to the kitchen to tell Fritz I was back, and then to the office. Even people who know better ask a lot of unnecessary questions—for instance, my asking Fritz if there had been any phone calls. In the first place, he would have told me without being asked, and in the second place, Cramer or Stebbins hardly ever phoned. They just came, and nearly always at eleven a.m. or around half past two, after lunch, or at six p.m., since they knew Wolfe's schedule. As I entered the office the elevator was whining down the shaft.

Wolfe walked in. Usually he goes to his desk before asking or looking a question, but that time he stopped short of it, glowered at me, and growled, "Well?"

"Well enough," I said. "What you would expect. Being set for a jolt is one thing and actually getting it is another. She was shying a little. She needed some assurance that you can stay in the saddle and I supplied it. She understands why she makes no exceptions when she's not answering questions. Purley asked her if she knew Ellen Tenzer. I assume we're standing pat."

"Yes." He crossed to the bookshelves and looked at titles. I had stopped long ago being nervous when his eyes went up to the two top shelves. If he decided to have another go at one of the books up out of reach he would get the ladder, mount it as high as necessary, and step down, and he wouldn't even wobble, let alone tumble. This time no title, high or low, appealed to him, and he moved to the big globe and started twirling it, slow motion. Presumably looking for a spot where the mother of a discarded baby might be hiding out, or perhaps for one where he could light when he had to blow town.

At dinnertime no company had come. There had been two phone calls, but not on official business. One was from Saul, reporting that two more names had been crossed off, and the other was Orrie. He had eliminated one more and had only two left. Fred was in Arizona. We were about to the end of the string.

At the table, when Wolfe finished his strawberries Romanoff, used his napkin, and pushed his chair back, I got to my feet and said, "I won't join you for coffee. They never come after dinner unless it's urgent, and I have a sort of a date."

He grunted. "Can I reach you?"

"Sure. At Mrs. Valdon's number. It's on the card."

He looked at me. "Is this flummery? You said she shied but you reassured her. Is she in fact in a pucker?"

"No, sir. She's set. But she may be afraid that you might pull out. She asked me to come and report after I spoke with you."

"Pfui."

"Yes, but she doesn't know you as well as I do. You don't know her as well as I do, either." I dropped my napkin on the table and departed.

Chapter 11

Cramer came at a quarter past eleven in the morning, Tuesday, July 3. When the doorbell rang I was on the phone, a purely personal matter. Back in May I had accepted an invitation to spend a five-day weekend, ending on the Fourth of July, at a friend's place up in Westchester. The marathon mother hunt had forced me to cancel, and the phone call was from the friend, to say that if I would drive up for the Fourth I would find a box of firecrackers and a toy cannon waiting for me. When the doorbell rang I said, "You know I would love to, but a police inspector is on the stoop right now, or maybe a sergeant, wanting in. I may spend the night in the jug. See you in court."

As I hung up the doorbell rang again. I went to the hall for a look through the one-way glass, and when I told Wolfe it was Cramer he merely tightened his lips. I went to the front, opened the door wide, and said, "Greetings. Mr. Wolfe is a little grumpy. He was expecting you yesterday." Most of that was wasted, at his back as he marched down the hall and into the office. I followed. Cramer removed the old felt hat he wears winter and summer, rain or shine, sat in the red leather

chair, no hurry, put the hat on the stand, and focused on
Wolfe. Wolfe focused back. They held it for a good five
seconds, just focusing. It wasn't a staring match; neither one had any idea he could out-eye the other one;
they were just getting their dukes up.

Cramer spoke. "It's been twenty-three days." He
was hoarse. That was unusual. Usually it took ten minutes or so with Wolfe to get him hoarse. Also his big
round face was a little redder than normal, but that
could have been the July heat.

"Twenty-five," Wolfe said. "Ellen Tenzer died the
night of June eighth."

"Twenty-three since I was here." Cramer settled
back. "What's the matter? Are you blocked?"

"Yes, sir."

"The hell you are. By what or whom?"

A corner of Wolfe's mouth went up an eighth of an
inch. "I couldn't answer that without telling you what
I'm after."

"I know you couldn't. I'm listening."

Wolfe shook his head. "Mr. Cramer. I am precisely
where I was twenty-three days ago. I have no information for you."

"That's hard to believe. I've never known you to
mark time for over three weeks. Do you know who
killed Ellen Tenzer?"

"I can answer that. No."

"I think you do. Have you any other client at present
than Mrs. Richard Valdon?"

"I can answer that too. No."

"Then I think you know who killed Ellen Tenzer.
Obviously there's a connection between her murder
and whatever Mrs. Valdon hired you to do. I don't need
to spell it all out—the buttons, Anne Tenzer, the over-

alls, the baby Ellen Tenzer had boarded, the baby in Mrs. Valdon's house, Goodwin's going to Mahopac to see Ellen Tenzer, her sudden departure after he had seen her. Do you deny that there is a direct connection between Goodwin's seeing Ellen Tenzer and the murder?"

"No. Nor affirm it. I don't know. Neither do you."

"Nuts." Cramer was getting hoarser. "You can add as well as I can. If you mean neither of us can prove it, okay, but you intend to. I don't know what Mrs. Valdon hired you to do, but I know damn well you intend to tag that murderer, *provided* it wasn't her. I don't think it was, because I think you know who it was, and if it was her you would have got from under before now. I can tell you why I think you know."

"Please do."

"I'm damn sure you would *like* to know. Do you deny that?"

"I'll concede it as a hypothesis."

"All right. You're spending Mrs. Valdon's money like water. Panzer and Durkin and Cather have been on the job for three weeks. They're here every day, and sometimes twice a day. I don't know what they're doing, but I know what they're not doing, and Goodwin too. They're absolutely ignoring Ellen Tenzer. None of them has been to Mahopac, or seen that Mrs. Nesbitt, or seen Anne Tenzer, or dug into Ellen Tenzer's record, or questioned her friends or neighbors, or contacted any of my men. They haven't shown the slightest interest in her, including Goodwin. But you would like to know who killed her. So you already know."

Wolfe grunted. "That's admirably specious, but drop it. I give you my word that I haven't the faintest notion of who killed Ellen Tenzer."

Cramer eyed him. "Your word?"

"Yes, sir."

That settled that. Cramer knew from experience that when Wolfe said "my word" it was straight and there was no catch in it. "Then what the hell," he demanded, "are Panzer and Durkin and Cather doing? And Goodwin?"

Wolfe shook his head. "No, sir. You have just said that you know what they're not doing. They're not trespassing in your province. They're not investigating a homicide. Nor Mr. Goodwin. Nor I."

Cramer looked at me. "You're under bail."

I nodded. "You ought to know."

"You spent the night in Mrs. Valdon's house. Last night."

I raised a brow. "There are two things wrong with that statement. First, it's not true. Second, even if it were true, what would it have to do with homicide?"

"What time did you leave?"

"I didn't. I'm still there."

He turned a hand over. "Look, Goodwin. You know I've got to depend on reports. The eight-to-two man says you entered at nine-twenty-five and didn't come out. The two-to-eight man says you didn't come out. I want to know which one missed you. What time did you leave?"

"I was wondering what you came for," I said. "I knew it couldn't be homicide, the way you were flopping around. So you're checking on the boys. Fine. By a quarter to two Mrs. Valdon and I were somewhat high, and we went out to dance on the sidewalk in the summer night. At a quarter past two she went back in and I left. So they both missed me. Also, of course—"

"You're a clown *and* a liar." He slowly raised a hand

and pinched his nose. He looked at Wolfe. He got a cigar from his pocket, glared at it, rolled it between his palms, stuck it in his mouth, and clamped his teeth on it. "I could get your licenses with a phone call to Albany," he said.

Wolfe nodded. "No doubt."

"But you're so goddam pigheaded." He removed the cigar. "You know I can get your license. You know I can take you down and book you as a material witness. You know you'll be wide open on a felony charge if you get stuck in the mud. But you're so goddam bullnecked I'm not going to waste my breath trying to put the screw on you."

"That's rational."

"Yeah. But you've got a client. Mrs. Richard Valdon. You're not only withholding evidence yourself, you and Goodwin, you have told her to."

"Does she say so?"

"She doesn't have to. Don't possum. Of course you have. She's your client and she's clammed up. The DA has asked her down and she won't go. So we'll take her."

"Isn't that a little brash? A citizen with her background and standing?"

"Not with what we know she knows. It was the buttons on the overalls that sent Goodwin to see Ellen Tenzer. The overalls were on the baby that Mrs. Valdon says was left in her vestibule and is now in her house. So—"

"You said Mrs. Valdon is mute."

"She told at least two people the baby was left in her vestibule—when she was alone in the house. She hasn't told us, but if she has any sense she will, if she's clean. She'll tell us everything she knows *if* she's clean, including what she hired you to do and what you've done. I don't think it was anything as raw as kidnapping because she had a lawyer make it legal on a temporary basis. But I'm damn sure the baby in her house is the one Ellen Tenzer had in *her* house until around May twentieth. There were two overalls in Ellen Tenzer's house exactly like the ones Goodwin showed to Anne Tenzer, with the same kind of buttons. Those goddam buttons."

It seemed to me beside the point for him to be nursing an anti-button grudge, but maybe he had had an interview with Nicholas Losseff.

He was going on. "So I want to know what Mrs. Valdon knows, and what you know, about that baby. The DA can't get anything out of her lawyer or her doctor, and of course they're privileged. The nurse and the maid and the cook aren't privileged, but if they know anything they've been corked. The nurse claims that all she knows about it is that it's a boy, it's healthy, and it's between five and seven months old. So Mrs. Valdon is not its mother. She didn't have a baby in December or January."

"I have given you my word," Wolfe said, "that I have no notion of who killed Ellen Tenzer."

"I heard you."

"I now give you my word that I know no more about that baby—its parentage, its background, who put it in Mrs. Valdon's vestibule—than you do."

"I don't believe it."

"Nonsense. Certainly you do. You know quite well I wouldn't dishonor that fine old phrase."

Cramer glared. "Then what in the name of God *do* you know? What did she hire you to do? Why have you kept her covered? Why have you told her to clam?"

"She consulted me in confidence. Why should I be

denied a privilege that is accorded to lawyers and doctors, even those who are patently unworthy of it? She had violated no law, she had done nothing for which she was obliged to account, she had no knowledge of an actionable offense. There was no—"

"What did she hire you to do?"

Wolfe nodded. "There's the rub. If I tell you that, with all details, or if she tells you, she will be a public target. When the baby was left in her vestibule it was wrapped in a blanket, and attached to the blanket inside, with an ordinary bare pin, was a slip of paper with a message on it. The message had been printed with rubber type—one of those kits that are used mostly by children. Therefore—"

"What did it say?"

"You're interrupting. Therefore it was useless as a pointer. It was the message that moved Mrs. Valdon to come to me. If I—"

"Where is it?"

"If I told you what it said my client would be subjected to vulgar notoriety. And it—"

"I want that message and I want it now!"

"You have interrupted me four times, Mr. Cramer. My tolerance is not infinite. You would say, of course, that the message would not be published, and in good faith, but your good faith isn't enough. No doubt Mrs. Nesbitt was assured that her name wouldn't become known, but it did. So I reserve the message. I was about to say, it wouldn't help you to find your murderer. Except for that one immaterial detail, you know all that I know, now that you have reached my client. As for what Mrs. Valdon hired me to do, that's manifest. I engaged to find the mother of the baby. They have been at that, and that alone, for more than three weeks—Mr.

Goodwin, Mr. Panzer, Mr. Durkin, and Mr. Cather. You ask if I'm blocked. I am. I'm at my wit's end."

"I'll bet you are." Cramer's eyes were slits. "If you're reserving the message why did you tell me about it?"

"To explain why Mrs. Valdon is at such pains about a baby left in her vestibule. To prevent her harassment I had to tell you what she hired me to do, and if I told you that, I had to tell you why."

"Of course you've got the message."

"I may have. If you have in mind getting a judge to order me to produce it, it will not be available. Don't bother."

"I won't." Cramer stood up. He took a step, threw the cigar at my wastebasket, and missed as usual. He looked down at Wolfe. "I don't believe there was a message. I noticed you didn't use that fine old phrase. I want the real reason Mrs. Valdon is spending a fortune on a stray baby, and keeping her lip buttoned, and if I don't get it from you, by God I'll get it from her. And if there was a message I'll get *that* from her."

Wolfe hit the desk with his fist. "After all this!" he roared. "After I have indulged you to the utmost! After I have given you my word on the two essential points! You would molest my client!"

"You're damn right I would." Cramer took a step toward the door, remembered his hat, reached across the red leather chair to get it, and marched out. I went to the hall to see that he was on the outside when he shut the door. When I stepped back in, Wolfe spoke.

"No mention of anonymous letters. A stratagem?"

"No. The mood he's in, he would have used any club he had. So it wasn't Upton. Not that that matters. There were a dozen lines to her."

He took in air through his nose, clear down, and let it

out through his mouth. "She knows nothing he doesn't know, except the message. Should you tell her to talk, reserving only that?"

"No. If she answers ten questions they'll make it a million. I'll go and tell her what to expect, and I'll be there when they come with a warrant. I suggest you should phone Parker. Tomorrow's the Fourth of July, and arranging bail on a holiday can be a problem."

"The wretch," he growled, and as I headed for the front I was wondering whether he meant Cramer or the client.

Chapter 12

When Saul Panzer phoned at half past three Saturday afternoon, July 7, to report that he had closed the last gap on the adoption, eliminating the girl who worked in Willis Krug's office, the second stage of the mother hunt was done. A very superior job by all five of us (I might as well include Wolfe): 148 girls and women covered and crossed off, and nobody's face scratched. Very satisfactory. Nuts. I told Saul that would be all for now but there might be more chores later. Fred and Orrie had already been turned loose.

Wolfe sat and scowled at whatever his eyes happened to light on. I asked him if he had any program for me, and when he gave me a look that the situation fully deserved but I didn't, I told him I was going to a beach for a swim and would be back Sunday night. He didn't even ask where he could reach me, but before I left I put a slip on his desk with a phone number. It belonged to a cottage on Long Island which Lucy Valdon had rented for the summer.

Cramer's bark had been worse than the DA's bite. She hadn't even had her name in the paper. When I arrived at Eleventh Street, Tuesday noon, and told her a caller would be coming she had a mild attack of funk, and she didn't eat much lunch, but when a Homicide Bureau dick came around three o'clock he didn't even have a warrant. Just a written request, signed by the DA himself. And when she phoned some four hours later she was already back home. The captain in charge of the bureau and two assistant DA's had each had a go at her, and one of them had been fairly tough, but she had lost no hide. The trouble with a clam is that you have only two choices: just sit and look at her, or lock her up. And she was an Armstead, she owned a house, she had a lot of friends, and the chance that she had killed Ellen Tenzer or knew who had was about one in ten million. So she spent the Fourth of July at the beach cottage with the baby, the nurse, the maid, and the cook. It had five bedrooms and six baths. What if the rooms are all occupied and a Homicide Bureau dick drops in and wants to take a bath? You have to be equipped.

Ordinarily, when I am out and away I forget the office and the current job, if any, and especially I forget Wolfe, but that Sunday at the beach my hostess was the client, so as I lay on the sand while she was inside feeding the baby I took a look at the prospect. One hundred per cent gloom. It often happens with the first look at a job that there seems to be no place to start, but you can always find some little spot to peck at. This was different. We had been at it nearly five weeks, we had followed two lines and come to a dead end both times, and there was no other possible line that I could see. I was about ready to buy the idea that Richard Valdon had not been the baby's father, that he had never met the girl who was its mother, and that she was some kind of a nut. She had read his books or seen him on television, and when she had a baby it wasn't convenient to keep, she had decided to arrange for it to be named Valdon. If it was something screwy like that, she was a needle in a haystack and the only hope was to forget the mother and go after the murderer, and the cops had been doing that for a solid month. At least ninety-nine per cent gloom. On my back on the sand with my eyes closed, I pronounced aloud an unrefined word, and Lucy's voice came. "Archie! I suppose I should have coughed."

I scrambled up and we made for the surf.

And Monday morning at eleven o'clock Wolfe walked into the office as if he were bound for somewhere, put the orchids in the vase, sat, and without glancing at the mail said, "Your notebook."

That started the third stage.

By lunchtime we had settled the last detail of the program and all that remained was to carry it out, which of course was my part. It took me only three days to get it set, but it was another four before the ball started to roll, because the Sunday *Gazette* appears only on Sunday. My three days went as follows:

MONDAY AFTERNOON. Back to the beach to sell the client on it. She balked and I stayed for dinner. It wasn't so much the moving back to town she objected to, it was the publicity, and it would have been no go if I hadn't stretched a point and mixed personal relations with business relations. When I left I had her promise to be back at Eleventh Street by Wednesday noon and to stay as long as necessary.

TUESDAY MORNING. To Al Posner, co-owner of the Posart Camera Exchange on 47th Street, to persuade him to come and help me buy a baby carriage. Back at his place with it, I left the selection of the cameras and their installation to him, after explaining how they were to be used, and he promised to have it ready by Wednesday noon.

TUESDAY AFTERNOON. To Lon Cohen's office on the twentieth floor of the *Gazette* Building. If Lon has a title I don't know what it is. Only his name is on the door of the small room, the second door down the hall from the big corner office of the publisher. I have been there maybe a hundred times over the years, and at least seventy of them he was at one of the three phones on his desk when I entered. He was that Tuesday. I took the chair at the end of the desk and waited.

He hung up, passed his hand over his smooth black hair, swiveled, and aimed his quick black eyes at me. "Where'd you get the sunburn?"

"I don't burn. You have no feeling for color." I patted my cheek. "Rich russet tan."

When that point had been settled, or rather not settled, I crossed my legs. "You're one lucky guy," I said. "Just because I like you, within reason, I walk in and hand you an exclusive that any paper in town would pay a grand for."

"Uh-huh. Say Ah."

"This is not a gift horse you have to look in the mouth of. You may have heard the name Lucy Valdon. The widow of Richard Valdon, the novelist?"

"Yeah."

"It will be a Sunday feature, full page, mostly pictures. A good wholesome title, maybe WOMEN LIKE BABIES. What text there is, there won't be much, will be by one of your word artists. It will tell how Mrs. Valdon, the young, beautiful, wealthy widow of a famous man, with no child of her own, has taken a baby into her luxurious home and is giving it her loving care. How she has hired an experienced nurse who is devoted to the little toddler—no, it can't toddle yet. Maybe the little angel or the little lambkin. I'm not writing it. How the nurse takes it out twice a day in its expensive carriage, from ten to eleven in the morning and from four to five in the afternoon, and wheels it around Washington Square, so it can enjoy the beauties of nature—trees and grass and so forth."

I gestured. "What a poem! If you have a poet on the payroll, swell, but it must include the details. The pictures can be whatever you want—Mrs. Valdon feeding the baby, or even bathing it if you like nudes—but one picture is a must, of the nurse with the carriage in Washington Square. I'll have to insist on that. Also it will have to be in next Sunday. The pictures can be taken tomorrow afternoon. You can thank me at your leisure. Any questions?"

As he opened his mouth, not to thank me, judging by his expression, a phone buzzed. He turned and got it, the green one, listened and talked, mostly listened, and hung up. "You have the nerve of a one-legged man at an ass-kicking convention," he said.

"That's not only vulgar," I said, "it's irrelevant."

"The hell it is. You may remember that one day a month ago, when you were here asking me about Ellen Tenzer, I asked you if you had found the buttons."

"Now that you remind me, yes."

"And you dodged. Okay, but now listen to you. You know more about the buttons than I do, but I know this much, they were on a baby's overalls, and Ellen Tenzer made them, and some of them were on baby's overalls in her house, and she had had a baby in her house, and the night after you went to see her she was murdered.

And now you come with this whimwham about Lucy
Valdon and a baby, and you ask if I have any questions.
I have. Is the baby in Lucy Valdon's house the one that
Ellen Tenzer had in hers?"

Of course I had known that would come. "Absolutely
off the record," I said.

"All right."

"Until further notice."

"I said all right."

"Then yes."

"Is Lucy Valdon its mother?"

"No."

"I don't ask if she's Wolfe's client, because that's
obvious. If she wasn't you wouldn't have her lined up
for your caper. As for it, the caper, I pass. No soap."

"There's no catch in it, Lon. She'll sign a release."

He shook his head. "That wouldn't help if someone
throws a bomb. It's a good guess that Ellen Tenzer got
murdered on account of that baby. That baby is hot, I
don't know why, but it is. You're asking me to put a
spotlight on it, not only where it lives, but where it can
be seen outdoors twice a day. That would be sweet. The
Gazette spots it, and the next day it gets snatched, or
run over and killed, or God knows what. Nothing doing,
Archie. Thank you for calling."

"I can tell you, straight, that there's no such risk.
None at all."

"Not good enough."

I uncrossed my legs. "Everything we have said is off
the record."

"Right."

"Here's more off the record. One will get you a thousand that there will be no snatch or any other trouble.
Mrs. Valdon hired Nero Wolfe five weeks ago today to

find out who the baby's mother is. It had been left in the vestibule of her house, and she knew nothing about it and still knows nothing. We have spent a lot of her money and our time and energy trying to find the mother, and have got nowhere. We're still trying. *This* attempt is based on the theory that a woman who had a baby six months ago and ditched it, no matter why, would like to see what it looks like. She will see the page in the *Gazette*, go to Washington Square, recognize the nurse and carriage from the picture, and have a look."

Lon's head was cocked. "What if she doesn't know the baby Mrs. Valdon has is hers?"

"She *probably* does. If she doesn't we're wasting some more time and energy and money."

"The *Gazette*'s circulation is nearly two million. If we ran that story there would be a mob of women around the carriage the next day. So?"

"I hope not a mob. There would be some, yes. The nurse will be a detective, the best female op around. You may have heard of her—Sally Corbett."

"Yeah."

"Saul Panzer and Fred Durkin and Orrie Cather will be on hand, within range. There will be three cameras attached to the carriage, not visible, and the nurse will know how to work them. They'll take shots of everyone who comes close enough for a look, and the pictures will be shown to Mrs. Valdon. Since the baby was left in her vestibule, it's a fair bet that the mother is someone she would recognize. The pictures will also be shown to a couple of other people whose names you don't need. Of course it depends on about a dozen ifs, but what doesn't? If you cross on the green you may get home alive. If you know what's good for your newspaper you'll grab this exclusive. If you run it and it works, you can have the picture of the mother and the story of how we got it, maybe."

"How straight is all this, Archie?"

"As straight as an ace, king, queen, jack, and ten."

"Who killed Ellen Tenzer?"

"How the hell do I know? Ask the cops or the DA."

"You say Panzer and Durkin and Cather will be on hand. Will you?"

"No. I might be recognized. I'm a celebrity. My picture has been in the *Gazette* three times in the last four years."

He lowered his head and rubbed his chin with a fingertip for five seconds. He looked up. "All right. The picture deadline for Sunday is eight a.m. Thursday."

It took an hour to get the details all settled because we were interrupted by four phone calls.

TUESDAY AFTERNOON CONTINUED. To Dol (Theodolinda) Bonner's office on 45th Street to keep a date with Sally Corbett, made on the phone that morning. Dol and Sally had been responsible, six years back, for my revision of my basic attitude toward female ops, and I held it against them, just as Wolfe held it against Jane Austen for forcing him to concede that a woman could write a good novel. That afternoon Sally showed me once again that I had to keep the revised version. She made only the notes that were necessary, she restricted her curiosity to her dark blue eyes, and she asked only the questions she had to. We arranged to meet at the Posart Camera Exchange in the morning.

WEDNESDAY MORNING. To the Posart Camera Exchange. Sally and I spent more than two hours in the workroom at the back with two mechanics, watching them install and test the cameras. They would have cost the client sixteen hundred bucks, but Al Posner was letting me rent them for a week. Sally was shown how to work them, but she would be fully coached later. I took her to lunch at Rusterman's.

WEDNESDAY AFTERNOON. To the Valdon house with Sally. Lucy had returned from the beach Tuesday evening. She had fixed it with the nurse, telling her that for a week or so someone else would take the baby out to give the nurse a break, and also with the maid and cook. I don't know how she explained the new fancy carriage, which was delivered before we arrived. By the time the *Gazette* personnel came, shortly before three—a lady journalist and a photographer with a helper—Sally was in her uniform, the nurse had gone for the afternoon, the carriage was outfitted, and Lucy needed a drink.

Newspaper photographers work fast, and he was through in the nursery, with Lucy and Sally, by half past three. I tagged along to Washington Square, to see how Sally handled a baby carriage. I hadn't made a study of that, but I thought she did all right, dragging her feet a little and letting her shoulders sag. When I got back to the house the lady journalist was still there with Lucy, but she soon went, and I made martinis.

THURSDAY, FRIDAY, and SATURDAY. To the *Gazette* first thing Thursday morning to look it over. The picture they had picked of Sally and the carriage, with baby, in the square, was perfect. The two of the nursery—one of Lucy with the baby in her arms, and one of Sally brushing the baby's hair with Lucy watching—were good enough shots, but Lucy's expression was not exactly doting. She looked like a woman trying to smile in spite of a toothache. Lon said the others had been even worse. I saw no point in using the one of the front of the house, but made no objection. Lon okayed the four changes I made in the text.

Sally wheeled the baby to Washington Square for its outing twice a day, all three days, but her camera instruction and practice took place in the house, in the big room on the second floor, with Al Posner and Lucy and me. Lucy was needed because she was seven inches shorter than me and all levels had to be covered. Two of the cameras were concealed in ornaments at the ends of the hand bar, and one was in a narrow box at the front of the carriage with a rattle and other trinkets. That one was worked by remote control. During those three days I had my picture taken at least a thousand times. The Thursday ones were mostly off focus, the Friday ones were better, and by Saturday morning Sally had it down pat. Anyone looking at the baby from a distance of six yards or less was going to get shot, and shot good.

Saul and Fred and Orrie were in the old brownstone Saturday evening until after midnight. They spent the first half-hour in the office getting briefed (Saul was to direct their deployment in the square in the morning), and the next three hours in the dining room with me, with refreshments, playing pinochle.

SUNDAY MORNING. To the kitchen for breakfast at nine-thirty. At ten o'clock, the moment when Sally would be entering the square pushing the carriage, I was starting on my third sour-milk griddle cake with my right hand, while my left hand held the *Gazette* open to the full-page spread entitled WOMEN LOVE BABIES. It's a matter of taste. In my opinion WOMEN LIKE BABIES would have been more subtle.

Chapter 13

When Lon Cohen said there would be a mob he had overrated something, perhaps the punch of the *Gazette*. The Sunday crop was twenty-six pictures, seven in the morning and nineteen in the afternoon. I was at the house when Sally returned with the carriage and its cargo a little after five, and helped her remove the films. There had been only two exposures with the camera in the box at the front of the carriage, but we rolled it through and took it. The way we were spending the client's dough, another couple of bucks was nothing.

Twenty-four hours later we still didn't know whether we had a picture of the mother or not. All we knew was that Lucy didn't recognize any of the twenty-six as someone she could name, and Julian Haft, Leo Bingham, and Willis Krug said they didn't. Wolfe had spoken to each of them on the phone in the morning, asking them to look at some pictures without explaining how we had got them, and when I got the prints from Al Posner around noon, six of each, I had sent packets by messenger. By five o'clock they had all phoned. Negative from all three. I took a set to Lucy and she gave them a good look. There was one she wasn't sure about, but the woman she thought it resembled had been on her list and had been eliminated by Saul. She invited me to stay until Sally took the baby on the afternoon outing and returned, and get the day's crop of films, but I wanted to be at 35th Street to get the reports from Krug and Haft and Bingham.

At twenty minutes past four Haft and Bingham had called but not Krug, and when the phone rang I supposed it would be him. But after the first word of the routine I was interrupted.

"Saul, Archie. A booth on University Place."

"And?"

"Maybe a break. Something we thought might happen. At four-oh-four a taxi stopped on the north side of the square, double-parked, and a woman got out. She crossed the street and looked around. The taxi stayed put. She spotted the carriage halfway across the square and headed for it and went right up to it. She didn't bend over or put a hand on the carriage or in it, but she spoke to Sally. She was there looking less than a minute—forty seconds. Orrie's car was around the corner, but with her hack waiting there was no point to that. She went back to it and it rolled. A Paragon. Do I stick here until five o'clock?"

"You do not. You find that hackie."

"Do you want the number?"

"Sure. You might get run over or something."

He gave me the taxi's registration number, and I jotted it down and told him I would be out from 4:45 to 6:00, getting the films from Sally and taking them to Al Posner. When I hung up I sat for a minute, breathing, enjoying it more than I had for weeks. Then I buzzed the plant rooms on the house phone.

"Yes?"

"Congratulations. Your theory that a woman who had a baby six months ago might like to see what it looks like was sound. The idea of having both the men and the cameras was also sound. I'm leaving in ten minutes and thought you might like to know. Two to one we have hooked the mother. Make it three to one."

"Please report."

"Glad to." I told him. "So if she's the mother we've got her. Finding out where the taxi took her may not help much, but of course Saul will know which picture. Congratulations."

"Satisfactory," he said, and hung up.

When Krug phoned a few minutes later, as I was getting up to go, to say that he didn't recognize any of the pictures I had sent him, he was probably surprised that I was so cheerful about it.

Monday's crop was more than twice as big as Sunday's, and Sally had changed the films at noon, so there were six rolls. Fifty-four exposures altogether, and one of them was worth its weight in rubies. I got them to 47th Street before six o'clock, but Al couldn't run them through that evening; two of his men were on vacation and one was home sick, and he was plugged up. I persuaded him to let me in at eight in the morning and took them home with me. While we were at the dinner table Saul phoned. The hackie's name was Sidney Bergman and he had welcomed a finif. He had picked up the fare on Madison Avenue between 52nd and 53rd Streets, taken her straight to the square, and back to 52nd and Park. He had never seen her before and knew nothing about her. I told Saul to keep an eye out for her at the square in the morning, she might come back for another look, and then come to the office and wait for me.

It was a quarter to twelve Tuesday morning when I got to the office with the prints. I could have made it half an hour sooner, but I had taken the time at the Posart Camera Exchange to make packets for Al to send to Krug and Haft and Bingham. If Lucy didn't know her, one of them might. Wolfe was at his desk with beer, and Saul was in the red leather chair with wine. A bottle of the Corton Charlemagne was on the stand at his elbow. Apparently they were discussing literature; there were three books on Wolfe's desk and one in his hand, open. I went and sat and listened. Yep, literature. I got up and started out and was stopped by Wolfe's voice.

"Yes, Archie?"

I turned. "I hate to interrupt." I approached Saul. "Feelthy pictures, mister?" I handed them to him.

"She didn't show this morning," he said. His hands were as deft with the prints as they were with a poker deck. A glance at each one was enough until he was about halfway through, when he tilted one for better light, nodded, and held it out. "That's her."

I took it. It was a good clear shot, three-quarter face, angled up as most of them were. Wide forehead, eyes the right distance apart, nose rather narrow, mouth rather wide, chin a little pointed. The eyes were fixed, focused to the right, concentrated.

"She could be attractive," I said.

"She is," Saul said. "She walks straight and smooth."

"Details?"

"Five feet seven. Hundred and twenty pounds. In the upper thirties."

"The envelope, please." He handed it to me, and I put the picture in with the others and the envelope in my pocket. "I'm sorry I had to interrupt you gentlemen. I have an errand. If you need me you know Mrs. Valdon's number." I turned and went.

Since Sunday, Lucy's relations with me had been a little strained. No, that's not good reporting. Her relations with the world were strained, and I happened to be handy. Her lawyer had phoned her Sunday evening about the *Gazette* piece, and he had come to the house for a talk Monday afternoon. He thought she was sticking her neck out and he strongly disapproved. Her best friend, Lena Guthrie, disapproved even more strongly, and she had had a dozen phone calls from other friends, not to mention enemies; and from a remark she made Monday afternoon I gathered that Leo Bingham had been one of them.

So there was an atmosphere, and when I arrived Tuesday and was directed by Marie Foltz to the second floor I had the big room to myself for nearly half an hour; and when the client finally came she stopped three paces short and asked, "Something new, Archie?"

"Just the prints," I said. "From yesterday."

"Oh. How many?"

"Fifty-four."

"I have a headache. I suppose I have to?"

"Maybe not." I got the envelope from my pocket, shuffled through the prints, and handed her one. "Try that one. It's special."

She gave it a glance. "What's special about it?"

"I'm betting three to one that she's the mother. She came in a taxi and had it wait while she spotted the carriage, went and took a good long look, nearly a minute, and went back to the taxi. Do you know her?"

Another glance at it. "No."

"Would you mind taking it to the light to make sure?"

"I don't— All right." She went to a lamp on a table

and switched it on, and looked, frowning. She turned. "I think I've seen her somewhere."

"Then forget your headache, all the headaches, and take another look. Of course we'll find her sooner or later, but it was six weeks ago today that you hired Nero Wolfe to find the mother, and we've spent a lot of your money, and you've had it fairly rough. It will save time and money and bumps if you can name her. Sit there by the lamp, huh?"

She closed her eyes and raised a hand to rub her forehead and went and sat. She didn't look at the print again, just sat and looked at space, frowning, with her lips pressed tight. Suddenly her head jerked around to me and she said, "Of course. Carol Mardus."

I laughed. "You know," I said, "during these six weeks I have seen you in various moods from gay to glum, but I have never seen you look really beat until this minute. I laughed because that's funny."

"I don't feel funny."

"I do. I feel wonderful. Are you sure it's Carol Mardus?"

"Yes. Certainly. It shouldn't have taken me so long."

"Who and what is she?"

"She got Dick started. She was a reader at *Distaff*, and she got Manny Upton to take Dick's stories. Then later he made her fiction editor. She is now."

"Fiction editor of *Distaff*?"

"Yes."

"She wasn't on your list."

"No, I didn't think of her. I've only seen her two or three times."

"C-A-R-O-L? M-A-R-D-I-S?"

"*U*-S."

"Married?"

"No. As far as I know. She was married to Willis Krug, and divorced."

My brows went up. "That's interesting. She wasn't on his list. Divorced how long ago?"

"I don't know exactly. I think four or five years. I only met her after I married Dick—and Willis too."

"I have to ask a question. If she's the mother, and now that's ten to one, how likely is it—no, not 'likely.' How credible is it that Dick was the father?"

"I don't know. I've told you about Dick, Archie. I know he had been intimate with her years ago—no, I don't *know* it, but someone told me. But if she's the mother—" Suddenly she was on her feet. "I'm going to see her. I'm going to ask her."

"Not right now." I started a hand for her arm but stopped it. Never mix personal relations with business relations unless you have to. "I'm going to give you an order. I've made a few requests and suggestions, and I've talked you into a couple of things, but I've never given you an order. Now I do. You will mention Carol Mardus to no one, positively no one, until I say you can. And you won't see her or phone her. Right?"

She smiled. "No one has ever given me an *order* since my father died."

"Then it's about time. Well?"

"Here." She put out a hand and I took it. The atmosphere was back to normal, but there was work to do.

"... client," I said, "you're the cream of the cream. I ... o use the phone on business."

... e was one in a cabinet at the end of the room, and ... and opened the door and dialed. I wouldn't have ... urprised if Fritz had answered, they were so ... n literature, but it was Saul. I told him it would save time if Wolfe got on, and in a moment had his voice. "Yes?"

"I'm at Mrs. Valdon's house. She knows the woman, not well. The name is Carol Mardus." I spelled it. "She's the fiction editor of *Distaff* magazine. The *Distaff* Building is on Madison Avenue at Fifty-second Street. She was intimate with Valdon some years ago. Further details to follow. Congratulations again. If she isn't the mother she certainly knows who is. I'm on my way, to find out what she was doing in January."

"No," Wolfe said. "Saul will go."

"Hold it. I slipped a cog." I turned to Lucy. "You said you've seen her two or three times. Did you see her last winter?"

She shook her head. "I was just thinking. I haven't seen her since Dick died."

To the phone. "Saul? Mrs. Valdon hasn't seen her since last September. Don't get too close to her, maybe she strangles the way she walks, straight and smooth. She was married to Willis Krug, but they were divorced four or five years ago. You might start with him, but you might not. He may not want to be reminded of her. She wasn't on his list. I have a suggestion."

"Yes?" Wolfe.

"Manuel Upton is her boss. He told you five weeks ago that if Mrs. Valdon wants a favor from him she can ask him. She could phone and ask him if Carol Mardus was around last winter. That might simplify it, but of course it might tangle it."

"It might indeed. Saul will follow routine. Tell Mrs. Valdon to mention Carol Mardus to no one."

"I already have."

"Tell her again. Stay with her. Divert her. Don't let her out of your sight." Click.

I cradled the phone and closed the cabinet. "Saul will check on Carol Mardus," I told Lucy. "My job is you. I am to keep you under constant surveillance. Mr. Wolfe understands you. He knows you wanted to find the mother so you could pull her hair. If you leave the house I'll have to tail you."

She tried to smile. "I *am* beat, Archie," she said. "Carol Mardus!"

"It's not certain yet, only ten to one," I told her.

Chapter 14

It became certain two days later, at twenty minutes past ten Thursday evening, when Saul made his last phone call from Florida.

Of course it was Ellen Tenzer that complicated it. If there had been nothing to it but the mother hunt, I could simply have gone to Carol Mardus, showed her the picture, and asked her how and where she had spent last winter; and if she had stalled I would have told her that it would be a cinch to find out if she had been carrying and having a baby, and she might as well save me time and trouble. But almost certainly, if she was the mother, she had either killed Ellen Tenzer or knew or suspected who had, so it wasn't so simple.

I ignored Wolfe's instruction to keep my eye on the client, women being the one thing he admits I know more about than he does, and took over for Saul at Washington Square. When I got to the office late Tuesday afternoon, after taking the day's crop of films to Al Posner, there had been developments. Willis Krug and Julian Haft and Leo Bingham had all phoned to say that they recognized none of the faces on the fifty-four prints, which was surprising in Krug's case, since he had been married to one of them. And Saul had phoned twice, first just before four o'clock, to get Wolfe before he went up to the plant rooms, to report that Carol Mardus had been absent from her job at *Distaff* for nearly six months, from Labor Day until the last of February, and again shortly after six to report that she had also been absent from her home, an apartment on East 83rd Street, and the apartment had not been sublet. That made it fifty to one. Wolfe enjoyed his dinner more than he had for weeks, and so did I.

A little before eleven the doorbell rang, and it was Saul. He preceded me to the office, sat in the red leather chair, and said, "I just did something I'm glad my father will never know about. I swore to something with my hand on the New Testament. The Bible was upside down."

Wolfe grunted. "Was it inescapable?"

"Yes. This person is a little twisted. He or she was taking fifty bucks to tell me something he or she had promised someone to keep secret, but first I had to swear on the Bible I would never tell who told me. That wasn't sensible. What if *my* price for telling was merely sixty bucks? Anyway I got the address." He got his notebook from a pocket and flipped it open. "Care of Mrs. Arthur P. Jordan, 1424 Sunset Drive, Lido Shores, Sarasota, Florida. Things sent there to Carol Mardus last fall reached her. He or she didn't swear to it on the Bible, but I bought it and paid for it."

"Satisfactory," Wolfe said. "Perhaps."

Saul nodded. "Of course it's still perhaps. There's a plane from Idlewild for Tampa at three-twenty-five a.m."

Wolfe made a face. "I suppose so." He hates airplanes. I suggested getting the Heron and driving Saul to Idlewild, but Wolfe said no, I was to be at Washington Square at ten in the morning. He knows how I yawn when I'm short on sleep.

Saul phoned four times from Florida. Wednesday afternoon he reported that 1424 Sunset Drive was the private residence of Mr. and Mrs. Arthur P. Jordan, and Carol Mardus had been a guest there last fall and winter. Late Wednesday evening he reported that Carol Mardus had been obviously pregnant in November and December. Thursday noon he reported that she had been taken to the Sarasota General Hospital on January 16, had been admitted under the name of Clara Waldron, and had given birth to a boy baby that night. At twenty minutes past ten Thursday evening he reported that he was at Tampa International Airport, that Clara Waldron, with baby, had taken a plane there for New York on February 5, and that he was doing likewise in three hours.

Wolfe and I hung up. The mother hunt was over. Forty-five days.

He eyed me. "How much of that woman's money have we spent?"

"Around fourteen grand."

"Pfui. Tell Fred and Orrie they're no longer needed. And Miss Corbett. Tell Mrs. Valdon she can return to the beach. Return the cameras."

"Yes, sir."

"Confound it! It could be so simple! But for that woman."

"The dead one. Yeah."

"But she gave you a drink of water."

"Nuts. If we emptied the bag for Cramer now, including the message, the only question would be should we demand separate trials. Not only you and me, also the client. I could ring Parker and ask him which is worse, withholding evidence or conspiring to obstruct justice."

He tightened his lips and took a deep breath, and another one. "Have you a suggestion?"

"I have a dozen. I have known for two days we would soon be facing this, and so have you. We can tackle Carol Mardus just on the mother angle, no mention of Ellen Tenzer, just what she did with her baby, and see what happens. There's a chance, a damn slim one but a chance, that she simply got rid of the baby, which isn't hard to do, and she didn't know what had happened to it, and that piece in the *Gazette* about Mrs. Valdon merely made her curious. Or suspicious. Second suggestion: we could take a stab at the rest of the commitment to the client. You were to learn the identity of the mother. Done. You were also to demonstrate the degree of probability that Valdon was the father. Before we tackle Carol Mardus head on we might do a routine job on her and Valdon in the spring of last year."

He shook his head. "That would take time and more money. You will see Carol Mardus."

"No, sir." I was emphatic. "You will. I saw Ellen Tenzer. I have seen Mrs. Valdon twenty times to your once. I'll do the chores, but it's your name on the billhead. In the morning?"

He scowled at me. Another woman to deal with. But he couldn't deny that I had a point. When that was settled I had another one, that there was no hurry about telling the client that the mother hunt was definitely over; it would be better to wait until we had had a talk with the mother herself.

Before I went up to bed I rang Fred Durkin, and Orrie Cather, and Sally Corbett, to tell them the operation was finished to Wolfe's satisfaction, not to mention mine. Also I considered dialing the number of Carol Mardus's apartment on 83rd Street, to invite her to drop in tomorrow morning, but decided not to give her a night to sleep on it.

I learned Friday morning that she *had* slept on it. I was intending to ring her at her office around ten o'clock, but at ten minutes to nine, when I was in the kitchen dealing with bacon and corn fritters with honey, the phone rang. I got it there in the kitchen and used the routine, and a woman's voice said she would like to speak with Mr. Wolfe. I said he wouldn't be available until eleven o'clock, and I was his confidential assistant, and perhaps I could help.

She said, "You're Archie Goodwin?"

"Right."

"You may have heard my name. Carol Mardus."

"Yes, Miss Mardus, I have."

"I'm calling to ask . . ." A pause. "I understand that inquiries are being made about me. Here in New York and also in Florida. Do you know anything about it?"

"Yes. They're being made at Mr. Wolfe's direction."

"Why does he . . ." Pause. "Why?"

"Where are you speaking from, Miss Mardus?"

"I'm in a phone booth. I'm on the way to my office. Does that matter?"

"It might. And even if you're in a booth I'd rather not discuss it on the phone. I shouldn't think you would, either. You went to a lot of trouble and expense to keep the baby strictly private."

"What baby?"

"Now really. It's much too late for that. But if you insist on an answer Mr. Wolfe will be free at eleven o'clock. Here at his office."

A longer pause. "I could come at noon."

"That will be fine. Speaking for myself, Miss Mardus, I look forward to seeing you."

As I hung up and returned to the corn fritters I was thinking, I certainly do. Long time no find.

When I had finished the second cup of coffee and gone to the office and done the chores, I buzzed the plant rooms on the house phone. If he didn't hear from me, Wolfe would be expecting to see her in the red leather chair when he came down, since he had told me to have her there at eleven o'clock, and he would appreciate knowing he would have an extra hour before he would have to dig in and work. He did. When I told him she had saved him a dime by calling herself and she would arrive at noon, he said, "Satisfactory."

I could use the extra hour too. Telling Fritz I was leaving on an errand, I went to Eleventh Street, told Lucy the Washington Square caper had been suspended and I would report at length later, removed the cameras from the baby carriage, took them to Al Posner, and told him to send a bill.

When the doorbell rang at ten minutes past noon and I went to the front, and at long last saw the mother in the flesh, my first impression was what the hell, if Richard Valdon played marbles with this when he had Lucy he was cuckoo. If she had been twenty years older it wouldn't have been stretching it much to call her a hag. But when I went to my desk and sat after steering her to the office and the red leather chair, I stared at her. It was a different face entirely that was turned to Wolfe. It had sugar and spice and everything nice—only "nice" may not be the right word exactly. She merely hadn't bothered to turn it on for the guy who opened the door. Also it wasn't exactly sugar in her voice as she told Wolfe how much she enjoyed being in his house and meeting him. Obviously the "I dare you" in both her voice and her eyes wasn't rigged; it had been built in, or born in.

Wolfe was leaning back, regarding her. "I can return that compliment, madam," he told her. "It gratifies me to meet you. I have been seeking you for six weeks."

"Seeking me? I'm in the phone book. I'm on the masthead of *Distaff*." The voice and eyes implied that she would have loved to hear from him.

Wolfe nodded. "But I didn't know that. I knew only that you had borne a baby and disposed of it. I had to—"

"You didn't know *I* had borne a baby. You couldn't have."

"I do now. While you were carrying it, the last four months, you were a guest at the home of Mrs. Arthur P. Jordan in Sarasota, Florida. You entered the Sarasota General Hospital on January sixteenth, as Clara Waldron, and the baby was born that night. When you boarded an airplane at Tampa, for New York, on February fifth, still as Clara Waldron, the baby was with you. What did you do with it and where is it now?"

It took her a moment to find her voice, but it was the same voice—almost. "I didn't come here to answer questions," she said. "I came to ask some. You've had a man making inquiries about me here in New York and then in Florida. Why?"

Wolfe pursed his lips. "There's no reason to withhold that," he conceded. He turned. "The picture, Archie?"

I got one of the prints from a drawer and went and handed it to her. She looked at it, at me, at the print again, and at Wolfe. "I've never seen this before. Where did you get it?"

"There were cameras attached to the baby carriage in Washington Square."

That fazed her. Her mouth opened, hung open a long moment, and closed. She looked at the print again, got its edge between thumbs and forefingers, tore it across, tore again, and put the pieces on the stand at her elbow.

"We have more," Wolfe said, "if you want one for a memento."

Her mouth opened and closed again, but no sound came.

"Altogether," Wolfe said, "the cameras took pictures of more than a hundred people, but yours was of special interest because you arrived at the square in a cab, expressly for the purpose of looking at the baby in that particular vehicle, having seen a picture of it, and the nurse, in a newspaper. You said—"

"My God," she blurted. "That's why she did that. *You* did it."

"I suggested it. You said you didn't come to answer questions, but it will simplify matters if you oblige me. Do you know Mr. Leo Bingham?"

"You know I do. Since you've made inquiries about me."

"Do you know Mr. Julian Haft?"

"Yes."

"And you know Mr. Willis Krug, since you were married to him. All of the pictures taken by the cameras were shown to those three men. Is one of them the father of your baby?"

"No!"

"Was Richard Valdon the father?"

No reply.

"Will you answer me, madam?"

"No."

"You won't answer, or he wasn't the father?"

"I won't answer."

"I advise you to. It is known that you were formerly intimate with Richard Valdon. Further inquiry will disclose if you renewed the intimacy in the spring of last year."

No comment.

"Will you answer?"

"No."

"When you arrived in New York with the baby on February fifth what did you do with it?"

No reply.

"Will you answer?"

"No."

"Did you at a later date leave the baby in the vestibule of Mrs. Valdon's house on Eleventh Street?"

No reply.

"Will you answer?"

"No."

"Did you print the message that was pinned to the baby's blanket when it was left in Mrs. Valdon's vestibule? Will you answer?"

"No."

"I strongly advise you, madam, to answer *this* question. How did you know that the baby Mrs. Valdon had in her house, as reported in the newspaper article, was your baby?"

No reply.

"Will you answer that?"

"No."

"Where were you in the evening of Sunday, May twentieth? Will you answer?"

"No."

"Where were you the night of Friday, June eighth? Will you answer?"

She got up and walked out, and I have to hand it to her, she walked straight and smooth. I would have had to double-quick to beat her to the front door, so I merely stepped to the hall. When she was out and the door was shut I stepped back in, returned to my desk, sat, and looked at Wolfe, and he looked back at me.

"Grrrr," he said.

"That last question," I said.

"What about it?"

"It may have been a little—uh—previous. It's barely possible, just barely, that she doesn't know about Ellen Tenzer. If the idea was to start her poking, shouldn't we have had Saul standing by? Or all three?"

"Pfui. Is she a nincompoop?"

"No."

"Then could even Saul shadow her?"

"Probably not. Then why ask her about June eighth?"

"She came here to find out how much we know. It was as well to inform her that our interest is not restricted to the baby and its parentage, that we are also concerned, even if only incidentally, with the death of Ellen Tenzer."

"Okay." I doubted if it was okay, but there was no point in pecking at it. "What comes next?"

"I don't know." He glowered at me. "Confound it, I am not lightning. I'll consider it. I shall probably want to see Mr. Bingham, Mr. Haft, and Mr. Krug, to ask why they failed to recognize her picture, though that may be inconsequential. I'll consider it. Will she approach Mrs. Valdon? Is she on her way there now?"

"No. Any odds you name."

"Is Mrs. Valdon in danger? Or the baby?"

I took five seconds and shook my head. "I can't see it."

"Nor can I. Report to her and tell her to return to the beach. Escort her. Return this evening. If you're anchored here you'll badger me and we'll squabble. Tomorrow we'll do something, I don't know what."

I objected. "Mrs. Valdon will want her own car at the beach. After reporting to her I'll have the afternoon and evening for checking on Carol Mardus for May twentieth."

"No!" He slapped the desk. "A jackass could do that. Have I no imagination? No wit? Am I a dolt?"

I stood. "Don't ask me if I'll answer. I might. Tell Fritz to save some lobster for me for when I come home tonight. The food at the beach is apt to be spotty." I went, first upstairs for a clean shirt.

So five hours later I was stretched out on the sand at the edge of the Atlantic. If I had extended an arm my fingers would have touched the client. Her reaction to the report had been in the groove for a woman. She had wanted to know what Carol Mardus had said, every word, and also how she had looked and how she had been dressed. There was an implication that the way she had been dressed had a definite bearing on the question, was Richard Valdon the father of the baby? but of course I let that slide. No man with any sense assumes that a woman's words mean to her exactly what they mean to him.

Naturally she wanted to know what we were going to do now. I told her if I knew the answer to that I wouldn't be there with her, I would be somewhere else, doing it. "The difficulty," I said, "is that Mr. Wolfe is a genius. A genius can't be bothered with just plain work like having someone tailed. He has to do stunts. He has to take a short cut. Anybody can get a rabbit out of a hat, so he has to get a hat out of a rabbit. This evening he will be sitting in the office, leaning back with his eyes closed, working his lips, pushing them out and pulling them in, out and in. That's probably how Newton discovered the law of gravitation, leaning back with his eyes closed and working his lips."

"He did not. It was an apple falling."

"Sure. His eyes were closed and it hit him on the nose."

When I got back to the old brownstone a little after midnight I was expecting to find on my desk a note telling me to come to Wolfe's room at 8:15 in the morning, but it wasn't there. Evidently his imagination and wit hadn't delivered. Fritz's had. In the kitchen there was a dish of Lobster Cardinal and a saucer with Parmesan ready grated. I sprinkled the cheese on and put it in the broiler, and drank milk and made coffee while it was browning, and while I was thinking that when Fritz came down after taking up the breakfast tray he might have word that I was to go up for instructions. Now that we had flushed the mother we had damn well better get a gun up.

Nothing doing. When Fritz returned to the kitchen at 8:20 Saturday morning, no word; and I had done with only six hours' sleep in order to be on tap. I decided to poke him, and it would be better to get him in his room before he went up to the orchids, so I speeded up with the poached eggs Creole and toasted muffins and skipped the second cup of coffee; and I was pushing my chair back when the phone rang.

It was Saul. He asked if I had listened to the 8:30 news, and I said no, I had been brooding.

"Then I'm bad news," he said. "About three hours ago a cop found a corpse in an alley off of Perry Street and it has been identified as Carol Mardus. She was strangled."

I said something but it didn't get out. My throat was clogged. I cleared it. "Anything else?"

"No, that was all."

"Thank you very much. I don't have to tell you to bite your tongue."

"Of course."

"And stand by." I hung up.

I looked at my watch: 8:53. I went to the hall, to the stairs, mounted a flight, found the door standing open, and entered. Wolfe had finished breakfast and was on his feet, shirt-sleeved, his jacket in his hand.

"Yes?" he demanded.

"Saul just phoned an item from the eight-thirty news. The body of Carol Mardus was found in an alley by a cop. Strangled."

He glared. "No."

"Yes."

He threw the jacket at me.

It came close, but I didn't catch it; I was too stunned. I couldn't believe he had actually done it. As I stood and stared he moved. He went to the house phone, on the table by a window, pushed the button, and lifted the receiver, and in a moment said in a voice tight with rage, "Good morning, Theodore. I won't be with you this morning." He cradled the phone and started pacing back and forth. He never paced. After half a dozen turns he came and picked up the jacket, put it on, and headed for the door.

"Where are you bound for?" I demanded.

"The plant rooms," he said, and kept going, and the sound came of the elevator. He was off his hinges. I went down to the kitchen and got my second cup of coffee.

Chapter 15

When Wolfe entered the office at eleven o'clock, assuming that he followed his schedule, he found on his desk a note which read as follows:

9:22 a.m. I am leaving for the beach, having phoned Mrs. Valdon that I'm coming. If she hears a news broadcast it might hit her as hard as it did you and she might do something undesirable. I'm assuming that we intend to hold on and will tell her so. I should be back by lunchtime. The phone number of the cottage is on the card.

AG

Actually the phone number was useless if he had something urgent to say, because at the moment he was reading the note I was in the Heron with the client beside me, parked under a tree at the roadside. There were two weekend guests at the cottage, in addition to the maid and cook and nurse, not a good setting for a strictly private conversation, and I had got Lucy in the car and away before telling her the news. Now, parked,

I could give her my whole attention, and she needed it. She had a grip on my arm and her teeth were clamped on her lip.

"Okay," I said, "it's tough. It's damn tough. All the ifs. If you hadn't hired Nero Wolfe I wouldn't have found Ellen Tenzer, and if I hadn't found her she wouldn't have been murdered. If you hadn't helped with that article in the paper and the baby-carriage act we wouldn't have found Carol Mardus, and if we hadn't found her *she* wouldn't have been murdered. But you have simply—"

"Do you *know* that, Archie?"

"No. I only know what Saul told me and what I heard on the radio on the way here. Just what I told you. But it's a million to one that that's why she got it. You have simply got to ignore the ifs. If you want to turn loose because of the risks you'll be taking if you don't, that might be sensible—"

"I don't want to turn loose."

I guess I gawked. "You don't?"

"No. I want Nero Wolfe to find him. To get him. The man who—the murderer—he killed both of them, didn't he?"

"Yes."

"He put the baby in my vestibule, didn't he?"

"Yes. Almost certainly."

"Then I want Nero Wolfe to get him."

"The cops would get him sooner or later."

"I want Nero Wolfe to get him."

I thought to myself, you never know. I had wasted my breath on the ifs; they were no longer bothering her. Maybe it was merely a matter of quantity; she could feel responsible for one murder but not for two. Anyhow, my errand had turned out to be quite different from what I had expected.

"Mr. Wolfe would certainly like to get him," I said. "So would I. But you're his client and you must understand that this changes the situation. On Ellen Tenzer we could claim that no connection had been established between her death and the job you hired Mr. Wolfe to do, and probably get away with it. Not on Carol Mardus. If we don't tell what we know about her, and the 'we' includes you, we are definitely withholding important evidence in a homicide case, and we couldn't claim we didn't know it was important evidence. Of course we know. So if we don't tell, and the cops dig it up themselves and get the murderer before we do, we're sunk. Mr. Wolfe and I would not only lose our licenses, we would also probably be sent up on a felony charge. You have no—"

"Archie, I don't—"

"Let me finish. You have no license to lose, but you would also be open to the felony charge. I doubt very much if they would press it, they probably wouldn't even charge you, but you would be wide open. I want to make that absolutely clear before you decide what to do."

"But you mean . . . you would go to jail?"

"Probably."

"All right."

"All right what?"

"I'll turn loose."

"Damn it, Lucy, you've twisted it all around. Or I have. We don't want you to turn loose. We positively don't. Mr. Wolfe is stiff with fury. He resented Ellen Tenzer being killed because he sent me to her, but that was nothing compared to this. If he doesn't nail the man who killed Carol Mardus he won't eat for a year. I

merely had to make it plain what you might be in for if
you stick."

"But you'll go to jail."

"That's my funeral. Also my business, I'm a detective. Leave that to us. The cops don't know there is any
connection between Carol Mardus and Ellen Tenzer
and you and us, and with any kind of a break they won't
know until we've got the murderer, and then it won't
matter. Have you mentioned Carol Mardus to anybody?"

"No."

"Positive?"

"Yes. You ordered me not to."

"So I did. I now order you to forget Mr. Wolfe and me
and think only of yourself. Do you stick or let go?"

She gripped my arm again. Her fingers were stron-
ger than you would expect. "Tell me honestly, Archie.
Do you want me to stick? Thinking only of yourself?"

"Yes."

"Then I stick. Kiss me."

"That sounds like an order."

"It is."

Twenty minutes later I turned the Heron into the
driveway, circled around the curve, and stopped at the
door of the cottage. No one was visible; they were all on
the beach side. As Lucy was getting out I spoke. "I just
had an idea. I have one a year. I might possibly be
walking past the house and feel like dropping in. May I
have a key?"

Her eyes widened. Nine hundred and ninety-nine
women out of a thousand, as things stood between us,
would have said, "Of course, but why?" She said only,
"Of course," swung the car door shut, and went. In a
couple of minutes she was back. She handed me the key,

said, "No phone call for you," and tried hard to smile. I pressed the gas pedal and was off.

One of the various prospects for the future that I didn't care for was sitting down for lunch with Wolfe. It would be painful. He always talked at table, and one of two things would happen. Either he would grump through it without even trying, or worse, he would pick something as far as possible from babies or murders, say the influence of Freud on theological dogma, and fight his way through. The prospect was bad enough without that. So I stopped at a place along the way and ate duckling, with a sauce that Fritz would have turned up his nose at, and it was five minutes to two when, after leaving the Heron at the garage around the corner, I mounted the stoop of the old brownstone and used my key.

Wolfe would be toward the end of lunch. But he wasn't. Not in the dining room. Crossing the hall to the office door, I glanced in. He wasn't there either, but someone else was. Leo Bingham was in the red leather chair, and Julian Haft was in one of the yellow ones. Their heads turned to me, and their faces were not cheerful. I beat it to the kitchen, and there was Wolfe at my breakfast table, with a board of cheese, crackers, and coffee. He looked up, grunted, and chewed. Fritz said, "The duckling's warm, Archie. Flemish olive sauce."

I swear I hadn't known duckling was on for lunch when I ordered it on the way. "I had a bite at the beach," I lied. To Wolfe: "Mrs. Valdon wants you to get the murderer. I told her the cops would get him sooner or later if she wanted to pull out, but she said, quote, 'I want Nero Wolfe to get him.' Unquote."

He growled. "You know quite well that that locution is vile."

"I feel vile. Do you know you have company?"

"Yes. Mr. Bingham came half an hour ago. I was at lunch; I haven't seen him. I told him through Fritz that I would not see him unless he got Mr. Haft and Mr. Krug to come, and he used the telephone." He was putting Brie on a cracker. "What took you so long? Was she difficult?"

"No. I dawdled. I was afraid to lunch with you. I thought you might throw your plate at me. Is Krug coming?"

"I don't know."

"You actually wouldn't have seen Bingham if he had balked?"

"Certainly I would. But he had to wait until I finished lunch, and he might as well try to get the others." He aimed a finger at me. "Archie. I am making an effort to control myself. I advise you to do the same. I realize that the provocation is as insupportable for you—"

The doorbell rang. I moved, but Wolfe snapped, "No. Fritz will go. Have some cheese. Coffee? Get a cup."

Fritz had gone. I got a cup and poured, and plastered a cracker with Brie. I was controlling myself. It might be Willis Krug at the door, but it might be Inspector Cramer, and if so, fur would fly. But when Fritz returned he said he had shown Mr. Krug to the office, and I took too big a sip of hot coffee and scalded my tongue. Wolfe took another cracker, and cheese, and then another. Finally he asked me politely if I wanted more, pushed his chair back, rose, thanked Fritz for the meal as always, and moved. I followed.

As we entered the office Leo Bingham bounced up

out of the red leather chair and boomed, "Who the hell do you think you are?"

Wolfe detoured around him. My route was between Wolfe's desk and the other two. Wolfe sat and said, "Sit down, Mr. Bingham."

"By God, if you—"

"Sit down!" Wolfe roared.

"I want to—"

"*Sit down!*"

Bingham sat.

Wolfe eyed him. "In my house I do the bawling," he said. "You came to see me, uninvited. What do you want?"

"I was invited," Julian Haft said. "What do *you* want?" His thin tenor was close to a squeak.

"I didn't come to go on the air," Bingham said. "You wanted Krug and Haft, and here they are. When you're through with them I'll speak with you privately."

Wolfe's head turned slowly to the right, to take his eyes past Haft to Krug, who was nearest me, and back again to the left. "It saves time," he said, "to have all three of you, because I wish to ask each of you the same question. And no doubt each of you would like to ask me the same question. Your question would be, why was a picture of Carol Mardus among those I sent you on Tuesday? My question is, why did none of you identify it?"

Bingham blurted, "You sent it to them too?"

"I did."

"Where did you get it?"

"I'm going to tell you, but with a long preamble. First, to clear the way, you should know that what I told you in this room nearly six weeks ago was pure invention. Mrs. Valdon had received no anonymous letters."

Bingham and Krug made noises. Haft adjusted his balloon-tired cheaters to stare better.

Wolfe ignored the noises. "It wasn't about anonymous letters that Mrs. Valdon came to me, it was about a baby that had been left in the vestibule of her house. She hired me to learn who had left it there and who its mother was. And father. I failed miserably. After a week of fruitless effort I decided to try the conjecture that Mrs. Valdon's late husband had been the father, and I asked her to get the cooperation of three or four of his close associates. You know how that resulted. Mr. Upton refused my request. Each of you three gave me a list of the names of women who had been in contact with Mr. Valdon in the spring of last year, the period when the baby had been conceived. I remark in passing that the name of Carol Mardus was on none of the lists."

"She's dead," Bingham blurted.

"She is indeed. Of course the procedure was to learn if any of the women listed had given birth to a baby at the time indicated. Four of them had, but the babies were all accounted for. That effort, again fruitless, took nearly four weeks. Close to desperation, I tried another conjecture, that the mother of the baby would like to see it, and I arranged for publication—but perhaps you saw the page in the *Gazette* about Mrs. Valdon?"

They all had.

"It worked. Hidden cameras were attached to the baby carriage, and pictures were taken of everyone who stopped for a look. That was the source of the pictures that were sent to each of you gentlemen on Monday and Tuesday. Each of you reported that he recognized none of them, but Mrs. Valdon recognized Carol Mardus and

named her. Inquiry disclosed that she had gone to Florida
last September, but remained there into the winter, had
entered a hospital on January sixteenth under an alias
and given birth to a baby, and had returned to New York
on February fifth, with the baby. Obviously I had found
the mother of the baby left in Mrs. Valdon's vestibule,
since the newspaper article had lured her to Washington
Square to look at it. Naturally I wished to see her, and
yesterday morning Mr. Goodwin was going to telephone
her, but she anticipated him. She phoned—when,
Archie?"

"Ten minutes to nine."

"And came shortly after twelve. She had—"

"She came *here?*" Leo Bingham.

"Yes, sir. She had learned that inquiries had been
made about her and wanted to know why. I told her,
and I asked questions, but she answered only three of
them—that she knew you, Mr. Bingham, and you, Mr.
Haft, and that neither of you, nor Mr. Krug, her former
husband, was the father of the baby. She sat there"—he
pointed to Bingham in the red leather chair—"while I
asked several other questions, but answered none of
them, and rose abruptly and departed. And now she's
dead."

No one spoke. Bingham was leaning forward, his
elbows on the chair arms, his jaw clamped, his eyes
fastened on Wolfe. Krug's eyes were closed. In profile
his long bony face looked even longer. Haft's mouth was
screwed up and he was blinking. From the side I could
see his eyelashes flick behind the cheaters.

"So that's why she . . ." Krug said, and let it hang.

"You've admitted you're a liar," Bingham said.

"You say she didn't answer your questions," Haft

said. "Then she didn't say she was the mother of the baby."

"In words, no. Implicitly, yes. I am being open. Since she is dead, and since Mr. Goodwin was present, we could give any account we pleased. I am reporting candidly. It is indubitable that Carol Mardus was the mother of the baby left in Mrs. Valdon's vestibule and that she was gravely disquieted to learn that I knew it and could demonstrate it. It is all but certain that some other person, X, was in some manner deeply involved, that she told X of her conversation with me, and that X, fearing that she would disclose his involvement, killed her. I am going to find X and expose him."

"This is . . . fantastic," Krug said.

"You may be candid," Haft said, "but it seems to me—what kind of involvement? He killed her just because he was involved in leaving a baby in a vestibule?"

"No. Does the name Ellen Tenzer mean anything to you, Mr. Haft?"

"No."

"To you, Mr. Krug?"

"Ellen Tenzer? No."

Bingham asked, "Wasn't that the name of the woman whose body was found in a car? Strangled? A few weeks ago?"

"It was. She was a retired nurse. She had boarded the baby that was left in Mrs. Valdon's vestibule, and Mr. Goodwin found her and spoke with her, and X killed her. The menace from Carol Mardus was not only that she would disclose his involvement with the baby, whatever it was, but that she knew he had murdered Ellen Tenzer."

"How did she know that?" Haft demanded.

"Presumably by inference. Presumably she knew

that her baby had been in the care of Ellen Tenzer. Presumably she read newspapers, and knew what had happened to Ellen Tenzer, and knew that Mr. Goodwin had gone to ask her about buttons on a baby's overalls, and knew that the police inquiry was centered on the baby she had recently boarded. As you see, I *am* being candid. I could simply say that Carol Mardus admitted this or that, and Mr. Goodwin would confirm it. I prefer to be open because I need your help."

"*Are* you open?" Bingham demanded.

"Yes."

"All this is straight—the baby, Lucy Valdon, Carol here yesterday, Ellen Tenzer?"

"It is."

"Have you told the police?"

"No. I'm—"

"Why not?"

"I'm about to go into that." Wolfe's eyes went right and left. "I have a proposal for you gentlemen. I'm assuming that you want the murderer of Carol Mardus brought to account, as I do. If I tell the police what I know I'll tell them *all* I know. I'll tell them of the lists of names you supplied me with—of course including the detail that Mr. Upton refused to supply one—and that the name of Carol Mardus appeared on none of them. I'll tell them of the pictures that were sent to you for identification, and that each of you reported that he recognized none of them, though the one of Carol Mardus was an excellent likeness. That will make it unpleasant for you, possibly even painful. The police are not witlings; they will know that each of you may have had a private reason for your reserve not relevant to their investigation; but they will also know that if one of you was involved with Carol Mardus regarding the baby, and if you killed Ellen Tenzer, you would certainly have omitted her name from your list and you would not have identified the picture. So they will be importunate with all of you."

"You seem to be saying," Krug said dryly, "that you are keeping all this from the police out of consideration for us."

Wolfe shook his head. "Not likely. I owe you no consideration at all, and you owe me none. But perhaps we can be mutually helpful. I would prefer not to help the police get the murderer because I want to get him myself, and I intend to. He has dared me with flagrant impudence. My client, Mrs. Valdon, gave me information in confidence, and I'll reveal it only under compulsion."

Haft had removed the cheaters and was fingering the bows. "You said you had a proposal."

"Yes. I can save you gentlemen severe annoyance by not telling the police what I know. In return you will answer some questions. Many questions. You may refuse to answer any specific one, but a refusal is often more informative than a reply. The point is, all of you will remain until I have finished. It may take hours. I don't expect to get all that is in your minds and memories regarding Carol Mardus, but I'll get all I can."

"You would probably get more," Krug said, "if you took us separately."

Wolfe shook his head. "This is better. What one omits another may supply. And it's safer, since it must be all or none. If one of you would rather answer to the police than to me, I withdraw the proposal. You, Mr. Krug?"

"I'll answer to the police anyway. I'm Carol's divorced husband. Of course the list and the picture would make it worse. And if you're as good as your reputation . . . I'll take you. I'll answer your questions."

"Mr. Bingham?"

"I'm in. I *may* answer your questions."

"Mr. Haft?"

He had the cheaters back on. "It seems to me all one-sided. You can tell the police about the lists and the pictures whenever you please."

"True. You risk that. I know I won't, if all of you accept my proposal, but you don't. Your choice is between a certainty and a possibility."

"Very well. I accept the proposal."

Wolfe swiveled to look up at the clock. Ten minutes to three. Good-by schedule. He couldn't possibly make it. He swiveled back. "It will take a while," he said. "Will you have something to drink?"

They all would, and Wolfe rang for Fritz. Scotch and soda for Haft, bourbon and water for Krug, brandy with water on the side for Bingham, milk for me, and beer for Wolfe. He leaned back and closed his eyes. Haft got up and crossed over to the bookshelves and looked at titles. Bingham asked to use the phone and then decided not to. Krug sat fidgeting, staring here and then there, lacing and unlacing his fingers. When his bourbon and water came he took some, had trouble with the swallowing, and nearly coughed it out. Wolfe opened the bottle of beer, dropped the cap in the drawer—they always go there so he can keep count—poured, watched the foam go down to an inch, and drank.

He licked his lips and focused on the divorced husband. "I have a suggestion, Mr. Krug. Tell me about Carol Mardus—your association with her, her association with others, anything that you think might be material. I'll interrupt with questions only if I must."

Chapter 16

Willis Krug took his time. He looked at Haft, not merely a glance, then at Bingham, and then at his glass, which was resting on his leg and had the fingers of both his hands curled around it. When he spoke his eyes stayed on the glass.

"There are people," he said, "quite a few people, who could probably tell you as much about Carol and me as I can. Maybe more for her part of it. We were married for exactly fourteen months. I wouldn't go through that again for . . ." He raised his eyes to Wolfe. "You know I was Dick Valdon's agent."

Wolfe nodded.

"Carol sent him to me. I had never met her or heard of her. She was a reader on *Distaff*, and she had persuaded Manny Upton to take three of Dick's stories, and she thought he should have an agent and sent him to me, and I met her through Dick, and we were married about a year later. I knew she and Dick had been—together. Everybody did. She had been with Manny Upton too. Everybody knew that too. I'm not speaking ill of the dead. She wouldn't think I was speaking ill of her if she were sitting here. She married me because she had been made fiction editor of *Distaff*, an important job, and she wanted—well, I'll use her words. She said she wanted to go tame. She was good with words. She could have made it as as writer."

He took some bourbon and water and was careful with the swallowing. "I thought she stayed tame for three or four months, but I didn't really know. I soon realized that with her you would never really know. I'm not going to name names because that was more than five years ago, and it wouldn't mean anything about the time you're interested in. I don't mean I'm not interested. I am. There was a time when I might have strangled her myself if I—if I had that in me. But that was long ago. You say you want to get the murderer—all right, I want you to. Of course I do. One thing hard for me to believe, that she had a baby. The way you tell it, she must have. She had an abortion while she was married to me. If she had a baby, Dick Valdon must have been the father, I'm sure of that. No other man ever meant to her what Dick did. God knows I didn't. Are you sure about the baby? That she went to Florida and had a baby?"

"Yes."

"Then Dick Valdon was the father."

Wolfe grunted. "I'm obliged to you, sir, on behalf of my client. Naturally the father's identity is of interest to her. Go on."

"That's all."

"Surely not. When was the divorce?"

"Nineteen-fifty-seven."

"And since then? Particularly the past sixteen months?"

"I can't help you on that. In the past two years I haven't seen Carol more than five or six times, at parties and so on. I've had some correspondence with her, and I've spoken with her on the phone fairly often, but only on business—manuscripts I sent her or wanted to send her. Of course I've heard talk about her. There are people who will say to a man, 'I understand your ex-wife is having a time with so-and-so.' That doesn't mean anything. Nothing those people say means anything."

"You're wrong, Mr. Krug. Every word uttered since man first invented words is a part of the record, though unrecorded. I grant that tattle is often vacuous. A question. If your association with your former wife has been only casual since the divorce, why did you omit her name from the list you gave me, and why did you not identify her picture?"

Krug nodded. "Of course." Pause. "Frankly, I don't know."

"Nonsense."

"It may be nonsense, but I don't know. Not putting her name on the list, that's easy to understand—" He stopped. A long pause. "No, I won't dodge it. It doesn't matter how I justified it consciously. We can't control our subconscious mind, but sometimes we know what it's up to. Subconsciously I refused to accept the possibility that Carol had sent anonymous letters to Lucy Valdon, so I didn't put her on the list and I tore the picture up. That's the best I can do, either for you or for the police."

"The police should never ask you. They will of course ask you this, so I might as well: did you kill Carol Mardus?"

"Oh, for God's sake. No."

"When and how did you learn of her death?"

"I was in the country for the weekend. I have a little place at Pound Ridge. Manny Upton phoned while I was having a late breakfast; the police had notified him and asked him to identify the body. Carol had no relatives in New York. I drove to town and went to my office, and I had only been there a few minutes when Leo Bingham phoned and asked me to come here."

"You spent the night in the country?"

"Yes."

"The police will want particulars, since you are the divorced husband, but I'll leave that to them. One more question, a hypothetical one. If Carol Mardus had a baby by Richard Valdon, conceived in April of last year and born last January, four months after Valdon's death; and if X knew about it, helped her dispose of it, and later, moved by pique or jealousy or spite, took it and left it in Mrs. Valdon's vestibule, who is X? Of the men in Carol Mardus's orbit, which one fits the specifications? I don't ask you to accuse, merely to suggest."

"I can't," Krug said. "I told you, I know nothing about her for the past two years."

Wolfe poured beer, emptying the bottle, waited until the foam was at the right level to bead his lips, drank, removed the beads with his tongue, put the glass down, and swiveled to face the red leather chair. "You heard the hypothetical question, Mr. Bingham. Have you a suggestion?"

"I wasn't listening," Bingham said. "I'm thinking about you. I'm getting tight on your brandy. I'm deciding whether to believe you or not, about how you got that picture. You're a very smooth article."

"Pfui. Believe me or not as you please. You accepted the proposal. What have you to say about Carol Mardus?"

Bingham hadn't had time to get tight, but he was working on it. Fritz had left the cognac bottle on the stand, and Bingham's second pouring had been a good three ounces. His neon-sign smile hadn't been turned on once, he hadn't shaved, and his necktie knot was off center.

"Carol Mardus," he said. "Carol Mardus was a fascinating aristocratic elegant tramp." He raised his glass. "To Carol!" He drank.

Wolfe asked, "Did you kill her?"

"Certainly." He drained the glass and put it on the stand. "All right, let's be serious. I met her years ago, and she could have had me by snapping her fingers, but there were two difficulties. I was broke and living on crumbs, and she belonged to my best friend, Dick Valdon. 'Belonged' is the wrong word because she never belonged to anybody, but she was Dick's for that year. Then she was somebody else's, and so on. Manny Upton, that fish. As you know, she was married for a while to Willis Krug." He looked at Krug. "You're no fish. Did you actually think she would go tame?"

No reply.

"You didn't. You couldn't." Bingham returned to Wolfe. "I used another wrong word. Carol wasn't a tramp. She certainly wasn't a floozy. Would a floozy leave a good job for six months to have a baby?"

"But you haven't decided to believe me."

"Hell, I believe you. I believe you because it fits Carol exactly. Krug's right, Dick was the father. And Dick was dead, so she could go ahead and have the baby. See? There wouldn't be a man it would belong to, it would just be hers. Then after it came she realized she didn't want it. She wouldn't be tied to a man, but it would be just as bad to be tied to a baby, only she didn't realize it until after it came. That's why I believe you, it fits her to a T. One thing I don't like, I admit it. You say someone helped her dispose of it, so she must have asked him to. Why didn't she ask me? That hurts. I mean that, it hurts."

He reached for the bottle with one hand and the glass with the other, poured, and took a healthy swallow. He wasn't appreciating the cognac, he was just drinking it. "Damn it," he said, "she should have asked me."

"Possibly she preferred to ask a woman."

"Not a chance. You can rule that out. Not Carol. Didn't it have to be kept secret?"

"Yes."

"She wouldn't have trusted *any* woman to keep *any* secret. She wouldn't have trusted any woman, period."

"You're hurt that she didn't ask you, that she didn't prefer you to the other available alternatives. So you must have some notion of who the other alternatives were. This question is not hypothetical; consider it established that she asked someone to help her dispose of the baby; whom did she ask, if not you?"

"I don't know."

"Of course you don't. But whom might she have trusted in so delicate a matter in preference to you?"

"You know, by God, that's a thought." Bingham put the glass to his lips and held it there. He took a little sip. "First I would say her ex-husband. Willis Krug."

"Mr. Krug says his only recent association with her has been on business matters. You challenge that?"

"No. I'm just answering your question. It's a damn good question. I know how Carol felt about Krug. She liked him. She felt he could be trusted, he could be depended on. But if he says it wasn't him it probably wasn't. My second pick would be Julian Haft."

Wolfe grunted. "You're merely naming those present. You're clowning."

"I am not. Carol thought Haft was the tops. She thought nobody was in his class as a judge of writing, and she let him know it. He was the only man she would have dinner with and then go home and read manuscripts. That's another reason tramp was the wrong word for her; she liked her work and was good at it. I can clown, but I'm not clowning now. But I shouldn't have put Krug first. I overlooked Manny Upton. He should be first."

"Her employer."

"Well, her boss. That's why he's first. He let her go for six months and come back to her job. He must have known what she went for. She told her friends, including me, that she was taking a long vacation, but she must have told Manny the truth. Hell, it's obvious. If you're half as good as you're supposed to be—it stares you in the face."

"It does indeed. But it was only yesterday afternoon that she was sitting in the chair you occupy. Granting that Mr. Upton is the most likely of the alternatives, are there any others? Besides Mr. Haft and Mr. Krug?"

"No." Bingham took a sip of brandy. "Not unless there was someone I didn't know about, and I don't think there was. Carol liked to tell me things. She liked the way I took things."

"I believe I asked you if you killed her."

"And I said certainly. I meant certainly I didn't. You haven't asked me where I spent last night and how and when I learned of her death. I spent the night at home in bed, alone, and I was at the studio before nine o'clock, at work. I'm getting up a pilot for a big fall show and I'm a month late. Someone at the studio heard it on the radio and told me. And there had been a picture of her in the batch you sent me Tuesday. I broke away as soon as I could and came to ask you about the picture. I knew damn well you must know something."

"So you recognized the picture."

"Of course I did. The reason I didn't say so, and I didn't put her on my list, was the same as Krug's, only he says his was subconscious and mine wasn't. You had told us you were looking for someone who had sent anonymous letters to Lucy Valdon. Carol Mardus couldn't possibly have sent anonymous letters to anybody. I didn't need my subconscious to tell me that."

"You were intimate with her, Mr. Bingham?"

"Balls. No, we were never on speaking terms. We used smoke signals." He looked at his watch. "I've got to get back to the studio."

"We should finish soon." Wolfe reached for his glass, emptied it, and put it down. "Mr. Haft. You are now conspicuous, on Mr. Bingham's roster of alternatives. I invite comment."

Haft was slumped in his chair with his spindly legs stuck out straight. Some men look all right slumping, but he wasn't built for it. He had finished his scotch and soda and put the glass on Wolfe's desk.

"I suppose I should feel flattered," he said. His thin tenor was quite a contrast to Bingham's full baritone. He turned his head to Bingham. "I appreciate it, Leo, your thought that Carol considered me worthy of her confidence on so delicate a matter. Even though you put me last, with Manny Upton first." He switched to Wolfe. "Since Bingham has accurately indicated the nature of my relations with Miss Mardus there seems to be nothing for me to say, except to answer for myself regarding the list and the picture. But on that too I have been anticipated. I can only parrot the others. Miss Mardus could not be guilty of sending anonymous letters. I believe that—No, you asked them about last night. Customarily I spend weekends at my home in Westport, but one of my most important authors, at least important to me, arrives this afternoon from England, and I'm taking him to dinner and the theater this evening. I slept in my suite at Churchill Towers, and I was there when Bingham phoned. I didn't know about Miss Mardus until he told me." He pulled his feet back. "Have you any questions?"

Wolfe was frowning at him. "What is the name of the important author?"

"Luke Cheatham."

"He wrote *No Moon Tonight.*"

"Yes."

"You publish him?"

"Yes."

"Please give him my regards."

"With pleasure. Certainly."

Wolfe looked at the clock. Twelve minutes to four. Plenty of time for a little speech. He surveyed them. "Gentlemen," he said, "we may not have mutual trust, but we have a mutual interest. Your professed reason for omitting the name of Carol Mardus from your lists and declining to identify her picture may or may not satisfy me, but it certainly wouldn't satisfy the police. They would suspect that for one of you it was false, and none of you can prove it genuine. So you don't want them to know what has been said here, or even that you have been here, and neither do I. That's our mutual interest. As for the outcome, we'll see. The man who killed Ellen Tenzer and Carol Mardus will inevitably be brought to account. For the reasons I gave you, I wish to be the instrument of his doom. With luck I will be."

He rose. "In any case, I am obliged to you on behalf of

my client." He headed for the hall, five minutes ahead of schedule. Leo Bingham looked at the brandy bottle, then at his watch, sprang to his feet, and went. I followed. In the hall Wolfe was entering the elevator. Bingham beat me to the front door, and I held it open because the other two were coming. They nodded as they passed by, and I stood on the sill and watched them down the stoop before I returned to the office.

There were several things to chew on, but of course the main one was Bingham's alternatives. If he had known Carol Mardus as well as he said he did there were just four candidates. Even if he had killed her himself, he would name the ones she would have been most likely to pick if she hadn't picked him, so it was highly probable that it was one of those four. I stood at a window, and sat at my desk, and stood some more, going over them. Which one? That's the silliest game of solitaire there is, and we all play it, trying to tag a murderer as one of a bunch from what they said and how they looked and acted, unless you can spot something that really opens a crack. I couldn't.

The trouble was, there was no telling how much time we had—a month or a week or a day. Or an hour. Homicide would check all angles on Carol Mardus, and they would all be seen and questioned, probably Willis Krug first, and one of them might wilt. If he did we were in the soup. There's a big difference between not giving information you haven't been asked for, and declining to give it, or faking it, when you *are* asked. All Cramer needed was a hint that there was a connection between Carol Mardus and the baby, or just that she had come to see Wolfe—anything at all that would bring him to the door, to march to the office and ask Wolfe if he had ever heard of Carol Mardus. That would do it. It was the thinnest ice we had ever been on. I had to go to the kitchen and chin with Fritz to keep from going up to the plant rooms and telling Wolfe that since he hadn't asked me before spilling it to Krug and Haft and Bingham, I wasn't going to ask him when and where I could spill it, and he could either fire me or quit fiddling with the damn orchids and do something. I decided to wait till he came down, and if he asked me if I had a suggestion I would throw something at him.

But he wouldn't find me in the office, sitting there like patience in the hoosegow. I would be in the hall and he could take it standing up. I wouldn't poke, I would punch. So when the sound came of the elevator I went out and took position facing its door, and when it jolted to a stop and the door opened, and he stepped out, he found himself confronted. As I opened my mouth the doorbell rang, and we both turned our heads for a look through the one-way glass. It was Inspector Cramer.

Chapter 17

Our heads jerked back and our eyes met. No words were needed, and no smoke signals. He muttered, "Come," and started to the rear, and I followed. In the kitchen Fritz was at the sink, sprinkling watercress with ice water. He glanced around, saw the look on Wolfe's face, and whirled.

"Mr. Cramer is at the door," Wolfe said. "Archie and I are leaving at the back and don't know when we'll return. Certainly not tonight. Don't admit him. Put the chain bolt on. Tell him we are not here and nothing else. Nothing. If he returns with a search warrant you'll have to admit him, but tell him nothing. You don't know when we left."

The doorbell rang.

"You understand?"

"Yes, but—"

"Go."

Fritz went. Wolfe asked me, "Pajamas and toothbrushes?"

"No time. If Stebbins is along he'll send him around to Thirty-fourth Street on the jump."

"You have cash?"

"Not enough. I'll get some." I hopped. But Fritz was opening the front door to the crack the chain bolt allowed, so I tiptoed to the office, to the safe, got the lettuce from the cash drawer, shut the safe door and twirled the dial, and tiptoed back to the hall. Wolfe was there, starting down the stairs. At the bottom I took the lead, on out, up the four steps, and along the brick walk to the gate with its Hotchkiss lock. Then through the passage to the 34th Street sidewalk. There was no point in stopping for a look around; it wasn't likely that Cramer had put a man there in advance, but if he had we would soon know it. We turned left. You wouldn't suppose that a man who does as little walking as Wolfe could stretch his legs without straining, but he can.

He can even talk. "Are we followed?"

"I doubt it. We've never done this before. Anyway we wouldn't be followed, we'd be stopped."

There was more sidewalk traffic than you would suppose on a July Saturday. We split to let a bee-line arm-swinger through and joined again. Wolfe asked, "Must it be a hotel?"

"No. Your picture has been in the paper too often. We can slow down when we're around the corner. I have a suggestion. At the beach this morning I had an idea that we might need a dugout, and I asked Mrs. Valdon for a key to her house. It's in my pocket."

"Isn't it under surveillance?"

"Why would it be? They went to the beach yesterday. There's no one there."

At the corner we waited for a green light, crossed 34th Street, and were headed downtown on Ninth Avenue. We let up a little. "It's under two miles," I said. "Exercise in the open air keeps the body fit and the mind alert. Hackies talk too much. For instance, one having a bowl of soup at a lunch counter says, 'Nero Wolfe is out. I just took him to that house on Eleventh Street where that woman's got that baby.' Within an hour it's all over town. We can stop at a bar for a beer break. Say when."

"*You* talk too much. You have seen me tramp through valleys and mountains for days."

"Yeah, and I'll never forget it."

We did stop on the way, at a delicatessen on Sixth Avenue and Twelfth Street, and when we entered the vestibule that had once lodged a baby in a blanket we were both loaded down. Ham, corned beef, sturgeon, anchovies, lettuce, radishes, scallions, cucumbers, oranges, lemons, peaches, plums, three kinds of crackers, coffee, butter, milk, cream, four kinds of cheese, eggs, pickles, olives, and twelve bottles of beer. No bread. If Fritz dies Wolfe will probably never eat bread again. It was ten minutes past seven when I got my arm unloaded enough, in the kitchen, to look at my watch, and it was a quarter to eight by the time I had things put away and Wolfe had dinner laid out on the kitchen table.

His salad dressing, from ingredients in the cupboard, wasn't as good as Fritz's, but of course he didn't have the materials. I washed the dishes and he dried.

There was now no point in punching or even poking. He was an exile from his house, his plant rooms, his chair, and his dining table, and there was only one way he could get back with his tail up. Of course I couldn't be sent on errands since I was an exile too, but there were Saul and Fred and Orrie, and presumably they were on his mind, where to start them digging, as we left the kitchen. But he asked me where the nursery was. I told him I doubted if he would find any clues there.

"The rug," he said. "You said there's a fine Tekke."

He not only inspected the Tekke, he looked at every rug in the house. Perfectly natural. He likes good rugs and knows a lot about them, and he seldom has a chance to see any but his own. Then he spent half an hour examining the elevator and running it up and down while I looked into the bed problem. A very enjoyable evening, but there was no point in poking. We turned in, finally, in the two spare rooms on the fourth floor. His had a nice rug which he said was an eighteenth-century Feraghan.

Sunday morning a smell woke me—at least it was the first thing I was aware of—a smell I knew well. It was faint, but I recognized it. I got erect and went out to the head of the stairs and sniffed; no doubt about it. I went down three flights to the kitchen and there he was, eating breakfast in his shirt sleeves. Eggs *au beurre noir*. He was playing house.

He said good morning. "Tell me twenty minutes before you're ready."

"Sure. Wine vinegar, I presume?"

He nodded. "Not very good, but it will do."

I went back up.

An hour and a half later, after eating breakfast and cleaning up, I found him in the big room on the second floor, in a big chair he had pulled over to a window, reading a book. I was still determined not to poke. I asked politely, "Shall I go out and get papers?"

"As you please. If you think it safe."

He wasn't playing house, he was camping out. You don't care about newspapers when you're camping out.

"Perhaps I should ring Mrs. Valdon and tell her where we are."

"That might be advisable, yes."

My valve popped open. "Listen, *sir*. There are times when you can afford to be eccentric and times when you can't. Maybe you can afford it even now, but not me. I quit."

He lowered the book slowly. "It's a summer Sunday, Archie. Where are people? Specifically, where is Mr. Upton? We are boxed up here. Will you undertake, using the telephone, to find Mr. Upton and persuade him to come here to talk with me? Supposing you could, would it be prudent?"

"No. But that's not the only line that's open. Who squawked to the cops? I might get that on the phone. That would make one less to work on."

"There isn't time for that approach. We can't shave, we can't change our shirts or socks or underwear. When you go for papers get toothbrushes. I must see Mr. Upton. I have been considering Mrs. Valdon. When you phone her ask her to come this evening, after dark, alone. Will she come?"

"Yes."

"Another detail I've considered. There's no hurry, but, since you're fuming—can you get Saul?"

"Yes. His answering service."

"Here tomorrow morning. I am considering Ellen Tenzer's niece. Anne?"

"Yes."

"If I properly understood her métier, she replaces office workers temporarily absent?"

"Right." My brows went up. "I'll be damned. Of course. It's certainly possible. I should have thought of it myself."

"You were too busy fuming. Speaking of fuming, the sturgeon is quite good, and I would like to try it *fumé à la Muscovite*. When you go for papers could you get some fennel, bay leaf, chives, parsley, shallots, and tomato paste?"

"At a delicatessen Sunday morning? No."

"A pity. Get any herbs they have."

A licensed private detective, and he didn't even know what you can expect to find in a delicatessen.

So the Sunday passed pleasantly—newspapers, books, television, all anyone could ask for. The sturgeon was fine, even with replacements for herbs temporarily absent. When I phoned Lucy and told her she had house guests and she was invited to come and spend the night with us, her first thought was sheets. Had there been any on the beds? Told that there had been, she was so relieved that our being fugitives from the law didn't really matter. Around nine o'clock Saul called, having got the message from the answering service, and I told him where to come in the morning. He had rung the office Saturday evening and again Sunday morning, having heard what had happened to Carol Mardus, and when Fritz had told him we weren't there and that was all he knew he had of course been a little *fumé*, knowing, as he did, that no limb was too long and narrow for Wolfe to crawl out on if he got peeved enough.

Not knowing if Lucy had another key, I stayed in the kitchen with a couple of magazines after supper, ready to answer the doorbell, but a little after ten o'clock I heard the door open and close and went to the hall to greet her. Needing two hands, or arms, for a satisfactory greeting between detective and client, she let her bag drop to the floor. That accomplished, I picked up the bag.

"I know why you're down here," she said. She looked very wholesome in a pale green summer dress and a dark green jacket. A well-tanned skin with a flush is more striking in town than at the beach. She took the bag. "You thought I might not be—discreet. You *are* conceited, but I like you anyway. Did you mean what you said on the phone? You and Nero Wolfe are actually *hiding?*"

I explained enough of the situation for her to get the idea, including what Krug and Bingham had said about Dick being the father of the baby. "So," I said, "the job you hired Mr. Wolfe for is done. All that's left now is a couple of murders, and if you want to get us out of your house just pick up the phone. The DA would be glad to send a car for us. It's been nice to know you. If I'm conceited you've helped it along. But first Mr. Wolfe would like to ask you something."

"Tell me the truth, Archie. Do you really think I might?"

"Certainly. You don't owe him anything. As for me, I'm not *that* conceited. I'm not actually conceited at all. I merely think it's common sense to like myself."

She smiled. "Where is he?"

"One flight up."

Wolfe left his chair when we entered the big room. An uninvited guest can at least be courteous. After exchanging greetings with him she glanced around, probably surprised that the place wasn't a mess with two men loose in it overnight. Then she told Wolfe she hoped he had been comfortable.

He grunted. "I have never been more uncomfortable in my life. No reflection on your hospitality is intended; I thank you heartily for the haven; but I'm a hound, not a hare. Mr. Goodwin has described the situation? Chairs, Archie."

I was already moving two of them up, knowing that

he would stick there with the roomiest one and the reading light. We sat.

Wolfe regarded her. "We're in a pickle. I ask you bluntly, madam, can you be steadfast?"

She frowned. "If you mean can I hold my tongue, yes, I can. I told Archie yesterday that I would."

"The police will press you, now that they have connected Carol Mardus with me and therefore with you, and I have decamped. You're my client and I should be shielding you, but instead you're shielding me. And Mr. Goodwin. He can thank you on his own behalf and no doubt will; for myself, I am deeply obliged, and I must ask you to extend the obligation. I need to see Manuel Upton as soon as possible. Will you get him here tomorrow morning?"

"Why—yes, if I can."

"Without telling him I'm here. He once told me that if you wanted a favor from him you could ask him. Very well, ask him to come to see you."

"And if he comes, what do I say?"

"Nothing. Just get him in the house. If I can't keep him in with words, Mr. Goodwin can with muscle. Do you like eggs?"

She laughed. She looked at me, so I laughed too.

Wolfe scowled. "Confound it, are eggs comical? Do you know how to scramble eggs, Mrs. Valdon?"

"Yes, of course."

"To use Mr. Goodwin's favorite locution, one will get you ten that you don't. I'll scramble eggs for your breakfast and we'll see. Tell me forty minutes before you're ready."

Her eyes widened. "Forty minutes?"

"Yes. I knew you didn't know."

Chapter 18

Manuel Upton came at a quarter to twelve Monday morning.

There had been a few little developments. The client had admitted to Wolfe, in my hearing, that she didn't know how to scramble eggs. I had admitted to him, in her hearing, that the scrambled eggs I had just eaten were fully up to Fritz's very best. He had admitted to her, in my hearing, that forty was more minutes than you could expect a housewife to spend exclusively on scrambling eggs, but he maintained that it was impossible to do it to perfection in less, with each and every particle exquisitely firm, soft, and moist.

The *News*, which I had to go out for, stated that the late Carol Mardus had once been a bosom friend of the late Richard Valdon, famous novelist, but there was no hint that that was anything more than an interesting item in her record which the public had a right to know.

Saul had come at half past nine as arranged, and had been instructed regarding Anne Tenzer. He had reported that he had phoned Fritz at eight o'clock, and had been told that Homicide dicks were holding down the office day and night, in shifts, by authority of a search warrant, and that one of them was listening in; and Saul had said that he was calling just to say that he had nothing on and was available for an errand if Wolfe had one. He also reported that he had heard from a reliable source—which he wouldn't name even to us—that a slip of paper with Wolfe's phone number on it had been found in Carol Mardus's apartment. So maybe no one had squawked. Maybe Cramer had merely been going to ask Wolfe if he had ever seen or heard of Carol Mardus, but that would have been enough to light the fuse. Saul was given three hundred dollars' worth of tens and twenties. Anne Tenzer might be broke and appreciate it.

The reception for Upton was simply staged. Lucy was tending door anyway, since there might possibly be an official caller for her, and she let him in, took him up to the second floor, and led him into the big room. I had moved the roomiest chair over near the couch, and Wolfe was in it. I was standing. Upton entered, saw us, and stopped. He turned to Lucy, but she wasn't there. She had slipped out and was shutting the door, as agreed.

Upton turned back to confront Wolfe. He was such a shrimp that with Wolfe sitting and him standing their eyes were almost at a level. He looked even smaller than I remembered. "You fat mountebank," he croaked. He wheeled and started for the door, found me in the way, blocking him, and stopped.

"Sorry," I said. "Road closed."

He had too much sense to argue with the help when it was obvious that the help would need only one hand. He turned his back on me. "This is absurd," he croaked. "This is New York, not Montenegro."

So, I thought, he's anti-Montenegro. I didn't say it, merely thought it, so it's not on my record.

Wolfe motioned to a chair. "You might as well sit, Mr. Upton. We're going to talk at length. If you mean it's absurd to hold you against your will, not at all. There are three of us to refute any accusation you might make. The handicap of your size precludes violence; Mr. Goodwin could dangle you like a marionette. Sit down."

Upton's jaw was set. "I'll talk with Mrs. Valdon."

"Perhaps, later. After you have told me all you know about Carol Mardus."

"Carol Mardus?"

"Yes."

"I see. I mean I don't see. Why do you—" He bit it off. Then: "You're here in Lucy Valdon's house. So you're still stringing her along. Have you sold her the idea that Carol Mardus sent her the anonymous letters? Now that she's dead?"

"There were no anonymous letters."

Upton gawked at him. There was a chair nearer to him than the couch, but he went to the couch and sat. "You can't get away with *that*," he said. "Three other men were there when you told us about the anonymous letters."

Wolfe nodded. "I've spoken with them again, Saturday afternoon, day before yesterday, and told them the anonymous letters were mere invention, invented by me to account for my request for lists of names. The lists didn't help any, but I have completed the job Mrs. Valdon hired me for. She no longer needs me; I am in her house only by her sufferance. I am now after a murderer. During my conversation with those three men Saturday afternoon the opinion was advanced that you killed Carol Mardus. That's what I want to discuss with you, the likelihood that you're a murderer."

"Blah." Upton cocked his head. "You know, I hand it to you. You've built a reputation on pure gall. Also you're a liar. No one advanced the opinion that I killed Carol Mardus. Did he say *why* I killed her? What are you really after? Why did you have Lucy Valdon get me down here?"

"To get some information I badly need. When did you learn that Carol Mardus came to see me on Friday?"

"More blah. I wouldn't have supposed you'd try that old worn-out trick—she came to see you, and she told you something, and she's dead. I suppose she told you I had threatened to kill her. Something like that?"

"No." Wolfe shifted in the chair. The back was too high for him to lean back properly as he did at home. "If we're to talk to any purpose I'll have to expound it. I engaged with Mrs. Valdon to find the mother of a baby that had been left in the vestibule of her house. I did so, at great expense and after much floundering about. It was Carol Mardus. She came to me on Friday to learn how much I knew, and I obliged her. To dispose of the baby when she returned from Florida with it, she had enlisted the help of a friend, a man. Call him X."

"Make it Z. X has been overworked."

Wolfe ignored it. "There were four men whom Miss Mardus might have gone to for help in such a matter: Willis Krug, Julian Haft, Leo Bingham, and yourself. Her choice, X, was not a happy one. The problem of the immediate disposal of the infant was well solved; it was placed in the care of one Ellen Tenzer, a retired nurse who lived alone in a house she owned in Mahopac. But Miss Mardus had told X that Richard Valdon was the father of the baby, and that was a mistake. For two reasons. There were two facts about X that Miss Mardus had not sufficiently considered: one, that he had himself been denied, and was still denied, the pleasure of her intimate favors, and resented it; and two, that he had the soul of an imp. Imp defined as a little malignant spirit. Being an editor, you know words."

Upton didn't say.

"So when the baby was four months old, and the expense of its upkeep made it desirable to dispose of it differently and permanently, X indulged himself in what he no doubt regarded as merely a prank. Choosing a Sunday in May because he knew Mrs. Valdon would be at home alone that evening, he got the baby from Ellen Tenzer, pinned to its blanket a slip of paper on which he had printed a message, deposited it in the vestibule of Mrs. Valdon's house, and telephoned her that there was something in her vestibule. The message is in my office safe. It said— Your memory is more exact than mine, Archie."

I was in the chair Upton had passed by. "Quote," I said. "'Mrs. Richard Valdon this baby is for you because a boy should live in his father's house.' End quote."

"Repeat it," Upton commanded me.

I repeated it.

"A little malignant spirit," Wolfe said. "He not only had the pleasure of perturbing Mrs. Valdon; there was the added fillip of telling Miss Mardus what he had done. But Mrs. Valdon came to me, and it took Mr. Goodwin and me just three days to learn that the baby had been in the care of Ellen Tenzer. Mr. Goodwin went to see her and spoke with her, and she was alarmed. I doubt if she knew how the baby had been disposed of; she probably didn't know who the mother was; but she did know that its origin was supposed to be a secret, never to be revealed. She communicated with X, and they met that evening. The soul of an imp is a strange phenomenon. It had led him to perform what he regarded as a permissible prank, but the threat of its imminent disclosure was intolerable. Permissible but not disclosable. He was with Ellen Tenzer in her car, and his strangling her was not on sudden impulse, for he must have had the cord with him."

Upton stirred on the couch. He was listening with both ears and both eyes. "I would give something," he said, "to know how much of *this* is invention. All of it?"

"No. Most of it is established or can be. Some, not much, is surmise on valid grounds. This next is surmise, for Miss Mardus did not tell me whether or when she had suspected that X had killed Ellen Tenzer. She must have suspected it if she knew that her baby had been in Ellen Tenzer's care, but she may not have known that. Did she read newspapers?"

"What?"

"Did Miss Mardus read newspapers?"

"Of course."

"Then it is not a surmise that after her talk with me she did suspect that X had killed Ellen Tenzer. More than a mere suspicion. The newspapers had reported Mr. Goodwin's visit to Ellen Tenzer. Must I elucidate that?"

"No."

"Then the rest is manifest. After her talk with me Miss Mardus did what Ellen Tenzer had done after her talk with Mr. Goodwin; she communicated with X. They met that evening, and he had a piece of cord in his pocket. Not, from the published descriptions, the same kind of cord he had used with Ellen Tenzer. A shrewd

precaution. The threat now was disclosure not merely
of a nasty prank, but of murder. He strangled her—this
time, perhaps, in his own car—and dumped the body in
an alley. An alley on Perry Street, less than a block
from the building where Willis Krug lives. Returning
her to her former husband? That's not even surmise,
merely comment. That would be suitably impish,
wouldn't it?"

"Finish it," Upton croaked. "Surmise who is X."

"That's risky, Mr. Upton. That might be slander."

"Yes. It might. Apparently they don't know any of
this at the District Attorney's office. I was there most
of yesterday. Shouldn't you tell them?"

"I should, yes. I haven't. I shall when I can name X."

"Then you're withholding evidence?"

"I'm doing something much worse; I'm conspiring to
obstruct justice. So are Mr. Goodwin and Mrs. Valdon.
That's why you must be detained until I can name X."

"You sit there and calmly . . ." Upton let it hang.
"It's unbelievable. Why me? Why are you telling me?"

"I needed to discuss it with you. I talked with Bingham and Krug and Haft on Saturday, and I wanted to
talk with you. One of them advanced the opinion, not
explicitly but by implication, that you had killed Carol
Mardus. His point was that you would not have let her
take a six months' vacation unless she confided in you
the compelling reason for it, that you knew she was
pregnant, and that therefore she had probably had your
help in disposing of the baby. Hence the conclusion that
you are X. Surely not wanton. When I said I wanted to
discuss the likelihood that you're a murderer you said
blah. I don't think you can dismiss it so cavalierly."

"I still say blah. And *I'm* not going to conspire to

obstruct justice." He stood up. "I *am* going to see if you'll actually . . ." He headed for the door.

Not having any great desire to dangle him, I merely beat him to the door and put my back to it. He made a grab for my arm, but missed and got the front of my jacket, and started pulling. That isn't good for a jacket, especially a light summer weight, and I got his wrists and twisted, maybe a little harder than necessary. He let go, so I did too, and the damn fool hauled off and swung. I sidestepped, whirled him around, pinned his arms from behind, hustled him across to a chair, and put him in it. That chair had been meant for him anyway. As I went to mine a ring came from the phone in the cabinet at the end of the room, but I ignored it.

Wolfe grunted. "Very well, you've established that you're under duress. So you're not conspiring. We'll assume that you are *not* X. But surely Miss Mardus told you why she had to have six months off. You knew she was pregnant and intended to give birth. Didn't she tell you later, when she returned, who had helped her dispose of the baby? You must see, Mr. Upton, that that is a question you must answer."

He was panting and glaring, at me. He moved the glare to Wolfe. "Not to you," he said. "I'll answer it to someone who has a right to ask it. And you'll have questions to answer, plenty of them." He stopped for breath. "I haven't mentioned the baby to the police because I didn't know it had any connection with her murder, and I don't know it yet. I have told them about the anonymous letters, and about your wanting lists of names of women who knew Dick Valdon, and that you probably got them from Krug and Haft and Bingham. If you think you can crawl—"

There was a knock at the door, and I went and opened

it enough to see out. Lucy was there. She whispered, "Saul Panzer," and I nodded, shut the door, and told Wolfe, "Phone for you," and he got up and came. I opened the door for him and shut it after him, returned to my chair, and sat.

"You were interrupted," I said politely. "You were saying something about crawling. If you want to go on I'll be glad to listen."

Apparently he didn't. He didn't even want to glare, and I knew why. His wrists were hurting and he didn't want to give me the satisfaction of seeing him rub them, and had to concentrate. When a wrist gets that particular twist it hurts for a while. I happened to know that there was a tube of salve in a cabinet upstairs that would have helped, but I wasn't going to take him up to get it. It wasn't my house, and anyway he shouldn't have jerked my jacket out of shape. Let him suffer. He did so, for a good fifteen minutes.

The door opened and Lucy entered, followed by Wolfe. She stopped and he advanced. Upton left the chair and started to speak, but Wolfe cut in. "Keep your seat. Mrs. Valdon is going to make a phone call, and you may as well hear her." He turned to me. "Tell her Mr. Cramer's number."

I did so, and she repeated it and headed for the cabinet at the end of the room. Upton moved in that direction but came up against me, and he told her back that Wolfe was a liar and a charlatan and so forth. When she got her number and spoke, he shut up and stood and listened. So did I. From the trouble she had getting Cramer, even though she gave her name, I guessed Lieutenant Rowcliff was on. I will never understand why Cramer keeps him around. But finally Lucy got him.

"Inspector Cramer? Yes, Lucy Valdon. I'm at home, my house on Eleventh Street. I have decided to tell you some things about the baby and about Carol Mardus. . . . Yes, Carol Mardus. . . . No, I don't want to tell the District Attorney, I want to tell you. . . . No, I don't know where Nero Wolfe is. I've decided I have to tell you, but I'm going to do it my way. I want to tell some other people too, at the same time. . . . Willis Krug and Leo Bingham and Julian Haft, and I want you to bring them or have them come. . . . That's right. . . . No, I won't do that, I want them to hear me telling you. . . . No, I won't, and I can be stubborn, you know I can, they have to be here with you. . . . No, Manuel Upton is here with me now. . . . That's all right, I'm all right. . . . Yes, I know exactly what I'm doing. . . . Of course, come right away if you want to, but I'm not going to tell you anything until they're all here. . . . Yes, certainly. . . . All right, I won't."

She hung up and turned. "Was that all right?"

"No," Wolfe said. "You shouldn't have told him Mr. Upton is here. He'll come first and want to see him. It's not important; you'll tell him he has gone. Archie, take him to the fourth floor and keep him quiet."

Chapter 19

In all the years I have been with Nero Wolfe that was the first and only time, to my knowledge, that he has been alone with a woman in a bedroom. The room was the one on the fourth floor he had slept in, and the woman was Anne Tenzer. I'm merely reporting, not insinuating; the door of the room was standing open, and not far away was another open door, to the room where I was keeping Manuel Upton quiet—but that gives a false impression. He was keeping himself quiet, needing no help from me. After hearing Lucy invite Inspector Cramer to call he hadn't uttered more than twenty words, and half of them had been to decline the offer of a ham sandwich and a glass of milk, brought up by Wolfe. I had accepted. Perfectly scrambled eggs are a fine dish, but they digest away on you.

Saul Panzer was downstairs helping Lucy receive and seat the guests, following instructions from Wolfe on the arrangement. He told me later that it was Leo Bingham, coming last, who held it up. It was twenty-five minutes to two when I heard footsteps and looked out and saw Saul at the door of the other room. He spoke to Wolfe, turned to me and said, "All set," and went to the stairs and started down. I ushered Upton out and into the elevator, and in a moment we were joined by Wolfe and Anne Tenzer. There would have been room for a couple more provided they weren't Wolfe's size. He pushed the button himself and cocked his head as we descended, listening for a creak or a groan, and hearing none. I suspected that before long I would be told to find out how much one like it would cost.

I have never thought that Inspector Cramer was a sap, and still don't. Take his reaction when he twisted his head around and saw us enter. He jumped up, opened his mouth, and shut it. He realized instantly that Wolfe wouldn't have dared to stage that charade if he hadn't had a line he was sure of, and if he blew his top in front of witnesses he might be just making it sweeter for Wolfe in the end. As we crossed to the group his face got redder and his mouth tighter, but he didn't let out a peep.

Saul had placed them as instructed. Lucy was off to the left, and near her was a chair for Anne Tenzer. Willis Krug and Julian Haft were on the couch, and Leo Bingham was on a chair at its right end. Cramer's chair was midway of the couch, facing it, and Saul was to his left. The roomiest chair, for Wolfe, was where I had put it earlier, near the left end of the couch, where there was space for Upton and me, putting Upton next to Haft and me not far from Wolfe.

But Upton had other ideas. When we reached the couch, instead of sitting he turned to face Cramer. "I want to enter a charge, Inspector," he said. "Against Nero Wolfe and Archie Goodwin. They have held me here by force, physical force. Goodwin assaulted me. I am Manuel Upton. I don't know what the charge is technically, but you do. I want you to put them under arrest."

Cramer had enough on his hands for the moment without that. He eyed him. "They're facing a more serious charge," he growled. He looked down at Wolfe, seated. "What about this one?"

Wolfe made a face. "Mr. Goodwin and Mrs. Valdon and I will flout it. I suggest that you act on it later, if at all. We have a graver matter to deal with—as you know, since obviously Mrs. Valdon's phone call was prompted by me."

"When did you come here?"

"Saturday. Day before yesterday."

"You've been here since Saturday?"

"Yes."

"Goodwin too?"

"Yes. Won't you sit? I don't like to stretch my neck."

"Arrest them," Upton croaked. "That's a formal demand. Arrest them."

"Don't be an ass," Wolfe told him. "I'm going to name a murderer, and Mr. Cramer knows it. Otherwise he would have arrested me, not on your charge, as soon as he caught sight of me." He looked around, right and then left. Cramer sat. I sat. That left Upton the only one on his feet, so he sat, between Haft and me on the couch.

Wolfe focused on Cramer. "I don't know how much you know, but gaps can be filled in later. This murderer is one of those unfortunate creatures who, neither designed nor fitted for that spectacular role, find themselves—"

"Save that for later too," Cramer growled.

"It's a necessary introduction. Find themselves abruptly rocketed into it. Some seven months ago Carol Mardus asked him to help her dispose of a baby she didn't want to keep, and he obliged her. If you had told him then that as a result of that amiable favor to a friend he would be twice a murderer within the year, he would have thought you were demented. The next fateful step, though not amiable, was not murderous; it was merely mischievous. Knowing that Richard Valdon had been the father of the baby, he took—"

"That's too big a gap. Was it the baby that was boarded by Ellen Tenzer?"

"Yes. I see this won't do. I must name him. Did you recognize the woman who entered the room with me?"

"No."

"She is Anne Tenzer, the niece of Ellen Tenzer. She was of course questioned in the investigation of her aunt's death, but apparently not by you." Wolfe turned. "Miss Tenzer, will you please tell Mr. Cramer what your occupation is?"

Anne cleared her throat. She was still a blonde, and if you asked ten men which of the two women sitting there was more attractive, her or Lucy, probably seven of them would say her. When she had entered the elevator and seen me she had said one word, hello, very offhand. Hello is not hi.

Her cool competent eyes went to Cramer. "I'm a secretary, with the Stopgap Employment Service. We fill in—vacations, any temporary vacancies. I'm at the senior executive level."

"So you have worked for many different firms?" Wolfe asked.

"I have worked *at* many different firms. My employer is the Stopgap Employment Service. I average about fifteen assignments a year."

"Is there anyone in this room you have ever worked for—on assignment?"

"Yes."

"Do you recognize him?"

"Certainly. Julian Haft, president of the Parthenon Press."

"When did you work for him?"

"I don't know the exact dates, but it was early last summer. I think it was the last two weeks in June and the first week in July."

"Did your work bring you into frequent contact with Mr. Haft?"

"Yes. I was replacing his private secretary. She was on vacation."

"Was the name of your aunt, Ellen Tenzer, ever mentioned in conversation with him?"

"Yes. He dictated a letter about a book, a manuscript, by a woman who had been a nurse, and I mentioned that I had an aunt who had been a nurse, and we talked about her a little. I must have mentioned that she boarded babies in her house sometimes, because when he called me up he asked—"

"If you please. When did he call you up?"

"Several months later, in the winter, I think some time in January. He called the Stopgap Employment Service and left a message, and I called him. He asked if my aunt still boarded babies, and I said I thought so, and he wanted her name and address."

"You supplied it? The name and address?"

"Yes."

"Have you been—"

"Just a minute." Cramer was glaring at her. "Why didn't you mention this when you were questioned at the time of your aunt's death?"

"Because I had forgotten—no, I hadn't forgotten, but I didn't think of it. Why should I?"

"What reminded you of it now?"

"A man came and asked me." She nodded at Saul. "That man. He named some men, four men, and asked if I had ever met any of them. I told him I had met Julian Haft, that I had worked for him, and he asked if I had any reason to suppose that he had ever heard of my aunt. Then of course I remembered, and I told him. He said it might help to find out who had killed my aunt, and I told him all about it."

"With him helping you to remember?"

"I don't know what you mean, 'helping me.' I do my own remembering. How could he help me remember?"

"He could make suggestions. He could suggest that you had told Mr. Haft that your aunt boarded babies. He could suggest the phone call that you say you received in January."

"Maybe he could, but he didn't. He didn't suggest anything, he just asked questions. It's you who are suggesting things. I'm doing something I'm not supposed to do, and I've never done it before. The kind of work I do, for lots of different men, important men, I'm not supposed to talk about it to anyone, and I never do. I'm talking about this because it's not really about my work, it's about my aunt, and she was murdered."

"Did this man pay you for the information you gave him?"

"No." Anne's eyes flashed and her chin jerked up. "I think you ought to be ashamed of yourself. My aunt was murdered more than six weeks ago, and you're the inspector in charge of murder cases, and you haven't arrested anybody, and when someone else tries to do something, and evidently he *has* done something, you accuse him of bribing *me*. You ought to be ashamed of yourself."

"I'm accusing no one, Miss Tenzer." Cramer didn't look ashamed. "I'm doing what this man did, asking you questions. Did he promise to pay you anything?"

"No!"

"Would you testify under oath to what you have said here?"

"Of course."

"Have you ever met or seen any of the other men in this room? Besides Mr. Haft?"

"No."

"You haven't? In the statement you signed some weeks ago, didn't you tell of a conversation you had had with one of them?"

She looked around. "Oh. Archie Goodwin. Yes."

"Have you seen Goodwin or spoken with him since the conversation you reported in that statement?"

"No."

"When did this man, Panzer, first see you and ask you questions?"

"Today. This morning."

"Had no one asked you any questions along this line before today?"

"No, I mean yes. No one."

Cramer's eyes went to Saul. "Panzer, do you confirm everything Miss Tenzer has said?"

Saul nodded. "I do. Everything I know about."

"You went to see her with instructions from Nero Wolfe?"

"I did."

"When and where did he give you the instructions?"

"Ask him."

"I'm asking you."

"Pfui," Wolfe said. "Tell him, Saul."

"In the kitchen in this house," Saul said. "Around half past nine this morning."

Cramer turned to Wolfe. "How did you suddenly get this idea about Anne Tenzer?"

Wolfe shook his head. "It wasn't sudden, it was tardy. Nor was it, properly speaking, an idea; it was merely a grab at a straw." He looked at Julian Haft. "I assume you recall the occasions described by Miss Tenzer, Mr. Haft? Last summer, a year ago, when she told you about her aunt, and last winter, when you phoned to get her name and address?"

Haft hadn't decided how to handle it. He must have been working at it ever since he had seen Anne Tenzer enter with Wolfe, but he had taken his cheaters off three times, and put them back on again three times, and if he couldn't decide what to do with his hands of course he hadn't decided what to do with his tongue. So he blurted. "No, I don't," he blurted.

"You don't recall those occasions?"

"No."

"Do you contradict her? Do you say she lies?"

He licked his lips. "I don't say she lies. I say she's mistaken. She must be confusing me with someone else."

"That's ill-advised. More, it's puerile. You should either acknowledge the facts she reports and challenge the implication, or call her a liar. But of course you're a dunce. You foolishly called attention to yourself that day in my office, back in June, when I told you and the others about the anonymous letters. You resisted my request for lists of names and were reluctant to give me one, but you asked to see the envelopes, saying that one of you might get a hint from the handwriting. That invited an assumption. Not the assumption that you had ground for a suspicion regarding the letters, for there were none, but that you knew there were none; and if you knew there had been no anonymous letters you—"

Cramer broke in. "You're saying there were no anonymous letters?"

"I am."

"That was all phony?"

"It was a maneuver. I told you gaps could be filled in later." Wolfe went back to Haft. "If you knew there had been no anonymous letters, and didn't say so, you probably knew what Mrs. Valdon had hired me to do. As I say, you foolishly called attention to yourself, but you incurred no real hazard since you had removed your link to peril by killing Ellen Tenzer. It would have—"

"That's a lie. I call *you* a liar."

"Of course. That would be imperative even for a worm, and by definition you're a man. You have nothing more to fear from me, Mr. Haft. I can't prove that you killed Ellen Tenzer and Carol Mardus; I can only declare it. I am satisfied. The job Mrs. Valdon hired me to do was completed two days ago, and she can't be expected to pay me to play Nemesis. Now that I have exposed you, your guilt and your impudence, I'll even offer advice. Leave here at once and prepare your defense. Of so extensive an operation there must be traces—letters or telegrams, check stubs and canceled checks if you paid Ellen Tenzer, a ball of cord, Ellen Tenzer's phone number jotted down somewhere, the rubber-stamp kit which you used for the message pinned to the baby's blanket, a hair from Carol Mardus's head in your car, a hair from your head in Ellen Tenzer's car—the possibilities are innumerable, now that you have been named. Also, of course, facts you can't erase, such as your use of a car, your own or another's, last Friday night. You have a job ahead of you, and you should get at it without delay. Go. Aren't you going?"

Leo Bingham muttered, "Good God, this is brutal."

"You know damn well he's not going," Cramer rasped. "Nobody is going." He stood up. "Where's a phone?"

Wolfe stretched his neck. "I have a suggestion. Two hours ago I asked Mr. Upton a question which he refused to answer. He said he would answer it to someone who has a right to ask it. I presume he would concede that you have the right. I suggest that you ask him if Carol Mardus told him who had helped her dispose of the baby."

Cramer glared at Upton. "Did she?"

"Yes," Upton said.

"Why the hell didn't you say so yesterday?"

"I wasn't asked. And I didn't know what I know now. I repeat my formal demand, that you arrest Nero Wolfe and Archie Goodwin on my complaint. But I'll answer your question. Carol Mardus told me that Julian Haft had met her at the airport, or right after she left it, and took the baby." He turned to Haft, beside him. "Julian, you can't expect me—" He didn't finish it. Haft was trying to take the cheaters off, and his hands were trembling so he couldn't manage it.

Cramer asked Mrs. Valdon, "Where's a phone?"

She pointed. "There."

He started for it but stopped and wheeled. "Stay where you are," he commanded. "All of you. I'm sending for cars and I'm taking you to the District Attorney's office." He focused on Wolfe. "Including you. You never leave your house, huh? Now that you've left it you'll go back when I say so." He headed for the cabinet.

Wolfe turned to the client. "Mrs. Valdon. You have indulged me and I am beholden to you. I suggest that you leave the room. Go upstairs and bolt the door. In Mr. Cramer's present temper he'll insist that you go along and there's no reason why you should. Please go."

Lucy got up and walked out. Forty-eight days had passed since she had walked out on me from that same room.

Chapter 20

At my breakfast table in the kitchen one morning last week, the kind of a snowy blowy January morning when it's nice to be inside a window looking out, I chewed slowly on my third bite of scrapple, swallowed it, and turned to Fritz.

"Creating again?" I asked.

He beamed at me. "You're learning to taste, Archie. To *distinguer*. In ten years more you'll have a palate. Can you tell me what I did?"

"Certainly not. But you did something. What?"

"I reduced the sage a little and added a touch of oregano. What do you think?"

"I think you're a genius. Two geniuses in one house, and one of them is easy to live with. You may quote me to the other one." I took a bite of scrapple, no bacon. Ordinarily I take bacon after the first two or three bites of scrapple, but I wanted to develop my palate. "Speaking of him, I suppose you've read the morning paper?"

"Yes. That murderer, that Haft, his appeal was denied."

"He'll try again. With money to pay lawyers you can

do a lot of dodging. That's one of the disadvantages of being poor, you don't dare kill anybody."

He was at the range, flipping the next slice of scrapple. "I'm sorry I kept you waiting, Archie, but the griddle was cold. I didn't expect you down until later. You said you were going to the Flamingo."

I swallowed scrapple and bacon. "Circling around again," I said. "You could just ask, why did I not go to the Flamingo, and if I did go why did I come home early."

"*Bien*. I ask."

"Good. I answer. First, I went. Second, I came home early because we left early. Third, why did we leave early. The baby had a temperature and my companion was worried about it. A worrying woman should not be dancing. Does that cover it?"

"Yes." He came and got my plate, and in a moment returned it with a slice of hot scrapple. "He is worried too, Archie. He thinks there is danger that you may marry that woman."

"I know he does. That suits me fine. In a month or so I can hit him for a raise." I took a bite of homemade scrapple with a touch of oregano.

The World of
Rex Stout

Now, for the first time ever, enjoy a peek into the life of Nero Wolfe's creator, Rex Stout, courtesy of the Stout estate. Pulled from Rex Stout's own archives, here is rarely seen, or never-before-published memorabilia. Each title in the Rex Stout Library will offer an exclusive look into the life of the man who gave Nero Wolfe life.

The Mother Hunt

A note from Rex Stout's publisher passing along praises from Britain for *The Mother Hunt*, with a question regarding page 11 of this edition, and a copy of the author's response.

Stout's directions for the much discussed scrambled eggs can be found in The World of Rex Stout section of *Where There's a Will*.

June 13 1963

TO THE PERSON WHO WROTE A LETTER IN
MAY TO CURTIS BROWN LTD. FROM WHICH
THEY QUOTED IN A LETTER THEY WROTE
ON MAY 31 to VIKING PRESS.

Dear Sir or Madam:

   1. My face is pink with pleasure
at your remarks about my "high standard"
and my latest book.

   2. The cheque Mrs. Valdon handed
Archie Goodwin (page 16, last line)
was for one thousand dollars. The
"00/100" merely shows that she knew
how to make out a check, American style.

                    Cordially,

THE VIKING PRESS INC • 625 MADISON AVENUE • NEW YORK 22 • NY

Memorandum

FOR ___MLB___   FROM ___EW___   DATE ___6/6/63___

THE MOTHER HUNT by Rex Stout

Copied from Curtis Brown Ltd. letter 5/31/63

Collins are delighted with his new novel THE MOTHER HUNT and write:

"It is wonderful what a high standard this writer manages to keep up in every single book. I have never had any direct communication with him and I would appreciate it very much, if and when you are in touch with him, if you would let him know how very highly we here think of him. We are delighted with his excellent new book, which will probably be published in January next year."

Perhaps you could pass these remarks on to him. Collins have also raised one small query about the text of THE MOTHER HUNT. "Page 10, last line – we don't understand quite what the size of the cheque was. It doesn't matter but it would be interesting to be enlightened about this by Rex Stout."

Dear Rex: Want to answer this yourself?
Like to know that your English publisher like you.

marshall